"I Want To Make Love To You."

Damon's voice was flat, his face expressionless. He could've been talking about something he didn't care that much about. Except she'd seen that hectic, passionate flash of emotion. And a telltale flame of fire still seared his cheeks.

"We can't."

"Why not?" he challenged. "And don't think you can come up with a reason I haven't already thought of and dismissed."

"You don't even like me."

"You're quite right. I didn't think I did."

She flinched, his honesty stinging. "So how can you even contemplate sleeping with me?"

"I must like something about you…to want you."

"Well, tough! You'll just have to live with the wanting because nothing is ever going to happen between us."

Dear Reader,

I've always loved books and can happily curl up with a book and read for hours. I love reading on Sunday afternoons when the winter rain beats against the windows. I love reading during summer vacations on the beach while the sun heats my skin and the soft sand warms my toes. There's something about escaping to another world, meeting people I've never known and being part of a slice of their lives that I find utterly compelling.

My favourite books suck me into the story and surprise me all the way through and, finally, leave me with a feeling of dizzy relief and delight. With my debut book, *Black Widow Bride*, I've tried to write the kind of story I love to read, and I hope you will visit me at www.tessaradley.com to find out more about what inspired me to write this book as well as my second Silhouette Desire novel, *Rich Man's Revenge*, which will be on sale this June.

Happy reading!

Take care,

Tessa

TESSA RADLEY

BLACK WIDOW BRIDE

Silhouette® Desire

Published by Silhouette Books
America's Publisher of Contemporary Romance

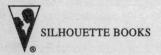

SILHOUETTE BOOKS

ISBN-13: 978-0-373-76794-6
ISBN-10:   0-373-76794-3

BLACK WIDOW BRIDE

Visit Silhouette Books at www.eHarlequin.com

Printed in U.S.A.

Books by Tessa Radley

Silhouette Desire

Black Widow Bride #1794

TESSA RADLEY

loves traveling, reading and watching the world around her. As a teen Tessa wanted to be an intrepid foreign correspondent. But after completing a Bachelor of Arts and marrying her sweetheart she became fascinated by law and ended up studying further and practicing as an attorney.

A six-month break traveling through Australia with her family re-awoke the yen to write. And life as a writer suits her perfectly; traveling and reading count as research and as for analyzing the world…well, she can think *what if* all day long. When she's not reading, traveling or thinking about writing she's spending time with her husband, her two sons—or her zany and wonderful friends. You can contact Tessa through her Web site www.tessaradley.com.

Dedications in first books are special. I've so many people to thank, so many people helped me along the way to selling that first book.

To writers and teachers—
To Daphne Clair and Robyn Donald for running the Kara School of Writing, without which I would never have plucked up the courage to write
And to Barbara Samuel for touching my heart and Emma Darcy for encouragement when I needed it most

To the editors who have helped me on my way—
Karin Stoecker for making me believe
Dianne Moggy for graceful advice and enthusiasm
Briony Green for her time and patience and excellent advice, which I will never forget

To my dream team—
Karen Solem and Melissa Jeglinski, who brought my dreams to life

To my writing group—
Karina Bliss, Abby Gaines and Sandra Hyde, friends and writers who fill my day with laughter

To my family—
Tony, Alex and Andrew, thank you for always believing and being there every day. You guys make each day special!

One

How had it all gone so horribly wrong?

Rebecca Grainger wrapped her arms around her stomach, nausea welling up. If she could only stop thinking about it, then maybe the sick feeling in the pit of her stomach would subside. The wedding was her priority, Rebecca told herself. Focus on that. She'd already been paid for arranging it—in full—the cheque flung at her last night.

Last night. That kiss. No, don't think about last night.

Concentrate on the wedding. An Asteriades event. A desperate glance swept the tables laden with glittering silver cutlery and Baccarat glasses, the slim crystal vases each bearing six glorious long-stemmed white roses on the tables.

Naturally she'd had unlimited resources at her disposal, and no expense had been spared for Damon Asteriades's wedding. The vaulted ballroom ceiling of Auckland's San Lorenzo Hotel had been draped in soft white folds of fabric to give the dreamy, romantic mood of a bower. Garlands of ivy and hothouse white roses festooned the walls, filling the ballroom with heady scent.

Brass wall-mounted sconces held torches that added an intimate glow, while the vast room had been heated to allow women to show off an astonishing array of flimsy designer gowns even though the winter air blew cold outside.

In the centre of the otherwise empty dance floor, Damon Asteriades performed a graceful manoeuvre, twirling his new bride to the melodious strains of the "Blue Danube" waltz, his dark head close to her pale blond hair. He was one hundred per cent gorgeous Greek male from the top of his overlong jet-black hair to the tips of his tanned fingers, with a Greek male's hotheaded certainty that he was always right. And right now Rebecca wished he were a million light-years away.

"My son is a fool."

At the voice of Soula Asteriades—Damon's mother and widow of the powerful Ari Asteriades—Rebecca smiled and said, "Damon wouldn't care for that description."

"And look at you, Rebecca! My dear, did you have to wear scarlet? Like a red flag to a bull?" Soula sighed. "That wicked dress will only fuel the tales that grow in each retelling."

Rebecca laughed and glanced down at the extravagant Vera Wang dress she wore. "Let them gossip. I don't care. At least I'm not stealing the bride's thunder and wearing white."

"But you should've been. You would've made a beautiful bride. If only Ari had been here—he might have knocked some sense into the boy's head."

Shocked, Rebecca stared at the older woman. *"Soula?"*

"This wedding is a mistake, but now it's too late. My son has made his choice and he must live with it. That's my last word." Soula disappeared into the throng surrounding them.

Disconcerted, Rebecca turned her attention to the dance floor. Damon chose that moment for an uncharacteristic display of public affection—brushing a kiss across the top of his bride's head. The bride tilted her face up, revealing astonishment but none of the sparkling joy expected. Rebecca couldn't help wishing that Damon was where she was right now—in hell.

She couldn't bear to watch. She closed her eyes. Her head ached with a combination of inner tension, the strain of the day and the residue of last night's wine. She wanted the wedding over. Done. So that she could rid her mouth of the bitter taste of betrayal.

"Come. Time for us to join them."

Rebecca's painful thoughts were jogged by a touch on her cold, clammy arm, and she became abruptly aware that the music from the stylish ensemble on the raised dais was fading. Savvas, the bridegroom's brother and best man, stared at her expectantly.

She forced a smile. "Sorry, Savvas. I was miles away." He gave her a wide grin. "Stop worrying, everything's magnificent. The flowers, the menu, the cake, the dress. Women will be queuing for you to organise their perfect day."

Rebecca blinked at Savvas's enthusiasm. Organising yet another Auckland high-society wedding was the last thing she wanted; yet she was thankful that he'd put her distraction down to anxiety about the success of the function. No one—not Savvas, nor anyone else—knew why she had fretted all day. Or why the memory of these particular nuptials would cast a pall over every wedding for years to come.

Oh, God, how could she have been so stupid last night!

"Come." Savvas tugged her hand insistently.

She dug her sandal-clad toes in, not budging. "I don't dance at weddings I've organised." Over Savvas's shoulder she met the bridegroom's narrow-eyed gaze, read the disdain.

It hurt.

More fool her. She dragged her attention back to Savvas.

He chuckled, oblivious to the tension that strung her tighter than the violinist's bowstring, his blue eyes lighting up with merriment, eyes so like his brother's that her heart jolted. No, she reprimanded herself, don't go there!

"No excuses. You're not working tonight, you must dance.

Come. It's traditional, the maid of honor and best man join in next. Look, everyone's waiting."

A rapid glance around told Rebecca he was right. Hordes of exquisitely dressed couples had flocked to the edge of the dance floor and stood waiting for them. Even Damon's mother was there, her eyes sympathetic. Rebecca raised her chin. Instinctively she touched the opal pendant that rested just above her breasts.

And then her gaze collided with blue. A cold, icy blue. Damon Asteriades was glaring now, disapproval evident in the hard slash of his mouth, his bride clamped in his arms.

His bride.

Fliss.

Her best friend.

Rebecca tossed her head, slid her chilled hand into the crook of the arm Savvas offered and, forcing a parody of a smile onto her lips, allowed him to lead her onto the floor, the flouncy skirt of her scarlet dress swirling around her legs.

She would dance. Damn Damon Asteriades! She would laugh, too, wouldn't let Damon glimpse the misery in her heart, the emptiness in her soul. Damon would never know what it had cost her to organise his wedding to Fliss, to help Fliss with the myriad choices of music, flowers, fabrics, or how sick and despondent she had felt trudging up the aisle behind the pair of them.

Nor would he ever know of her quiet desperation when the white-and-gold-robed priest had pronounced them man and wife. Of the ache that had sharpened as the bridal couple had turned to face the congregation. Fliss had been pale, but she'd managed to give Damon a flirtatious glance from under her lashes. And Damon had sought Rebecca's gaze, his eyes blazing with triumph, as if to say, Nothing you can do now.

Oh, yes, she'd dance. She'd be as outrageous as ever, and not a soul would guess at the agony hidden beneath the brittle facade. They'd see what they always saw: brazen, independent Rebecca.

Never again would she allow herself to become vulnerable to this raw, consuming emotion. It hurt too much.

She smiled determinedly up at Savvas as he put an arm around her shoulder and ignored the glower from the midst of the dance floor.

"Hey, brother, my turn to dance with the bride."

Startled by Savvas's words, Rebecca surfaced from the numb place to which she'd retreated, a place where she felt nothing. No pain, no emotion. The sudden stop brought her back to the present, back to the ballroom. Savvas stepped away as the romantic melody faded.

In front of her stood her nemesis, the man she knew she would never escape.

Even in this dim light his blue gaze glittered. Only the bent blade of a nose that had clearly been broken more than once saved his face from the classic beauty his full mouth and impossibly high cheekbones promised. Instead it created a face filled with danger, utterly compelling and ruthlessly sensual. A modern-day pirate.

Hastily she looked away, grabbing for her departing dance partner.

"Savvas?"

But Savvas was gone, spinning Fliss away, Fliss's wedding dress fanning out against his legs. Feeling utterly alone, Rebecca waited, heart thudding with apprehension, refusing to look at Damon.

"So, you are now trying to seduce my brother? Another crack at the Asteriades fortune, hmm?" Her head shot back at the cynical words. There was something dark and tumultuous in his eyes.

He was angry?

What about *her*?

What gave him the right to judge her? He didn't even know her—hadn't had the slightest inclination to get to know her.

"Go to hell," she muttered through grimly smiling teeth and swung away.

"Oh, no, Rebecca." A hard hand caught her elbow. "It's not going to be that easy. I'm not going to allow you to cause a scene and leave me standing alone on the dance floor. You're not making a fool of me."

Rebecca tried to wrench free. The grip tightened. Big. Strong. Powerful. She didn't have a hope of escaping Damon Asteriades. But the last thing in the world she wanted today was to be held in his arms, to dance with him.

No.

She must have said it aloud, because his mouth flattened as he twirled her around to face him.

"Yes," he hissed. His eyes had turned to flat, unforgiving cobalt chips. "You will dance with me." His right hand moved to rest on her waist as the joyous bars of the next waltz struck up. "For once in your selfish life you will do something for someone else. I will not allow you to destroy Felicity's day."

As he'd already destroyed her.

Rebecca wanted to laugh hysterically. Damon had no idea…no idea that he would destroy Fliss, too. Dear, beloved Fliss, the closest thing she had to a sister. Her best friend. Her business partner. Or at least she had been until last night when, after the final wedding rehearsal, Fliss had signed her share in Dream Occasions over to Rebecca.

And why? Because Damon had demanded it.

The lord and master had made it clear he wanted all ties to Rebecca severed, and Fliss had obeyed. Rebecca had been hotly, impulsively furious. Yet under the fury there had simmered the unspeakable pain of betrayal. Rebecca knew why Fliss had capitulated. Hell, she even understood why her friend was so desperate to marry a man to whom she was so totally unsuited.

But Fliss should've known better, should *never* have agreed to marry him. Yet how could Fliss refuse? Because Fliss craved security—as Rebecca once had. Unlike a heroine tied to the train tracks in one of those ancient black-and-white movies, Fliss didn't see the danger. She saw only Damon's solid strength. His power and wealth.

Damon was too strong. He'd dominate her. Fliss would never stand up to him. Rebecca feared Fliss would wither and die. So last night Rebecca had decided to take matters into her own hands.

A cold line of goose bumps swept her spine. Rebecca gave a convulsive shiver at the memory of what had happened next.

And afterward…

God! She would *never* forget the thrust of Damon's anger, his contempt…or his furious passion…as long as she lived. Not even the gallons of red wine she'd consumed later had dimmed the pain, the knowledge of what that one last desperate shot had cost.

"Fliss," she said gently as Damon's hand enfolded hers—trapping her—as he led her into the waltz.

Damon glared down at her, uncomprehending.

"She likes to be called Fliss. Or hasn't she told you that yet?"

His black eyebrows drew together, and she was terribly aware of the heat of his hand on her waist, of the intimate pressure of his palm against hers, of his hot, sexy scent.

"Her name is Felicity," he said repressively. "It's beautiful. A happy name. The other sounds insubstantial, like fairy floss."

"But she hates it. Or don't her wishes matter to you?"

The name reminded Fliss of less happy times, of a childhood where she'd been shy, small for her age—of the bullying she'd endured at school as the child of a foster home, of the stark discipline meted out by foster parents who had their own two daughters to love. Rebecca knew because she'd been there, raised by the same distant but well-meaning couple. How could she explain it to Damon? She couldn't! Rebecca reminded herself she was no longer the rock in Fliss's life. It was up to Fliss to tell her husband what she chose.

Momentarily Damon looked taken aback, but already his face was hardening. "It has nothing to do with you what I call my wife. All I ask is that you refrain from ruining this day."

My wife.

Again the agonising sharpness pierced her heart. Rebecca pushed the pain away. She'd deal with it later, much later, when this appalling day was over and she was alone.

"And how would I do that?" She raised a brow, pretending an insouciance she was far from feeling, here, trapped within the heat of his arms, mindless of the other dancing couples surrounding them. "Savvas told me that everything is stunning— the flowers…the wedding dress…the wedding cake—that it's a Dream Occasion. How could I possibly *ruin* it?" Each word she uttered was another blow to her already battered heart.

But he didn't smile at her intentional pun on her business's name. Instead his glower darkened. "Don't be obtuse. I'm not doubting your professional ability, it's your penchant for stirring up trouble that has me worried."

If only she could hate him.

Damon despised her. And, at this moment, she didn't like him much either. To be quite honest, more than anything in the world she wanted to kill Damon Asteriades, business tycoon, billionaire…and the blindest, most stubborn, most controlling man she'd ever met. If he'd been more attuned to her, he would've known that Fliss would be safe, that there'd be no catfight on the dance floor tonight. Rebellion stirred within Rebecca. Perhaps she should give him cause to worry. Punish him a little.

She gave her slowest, most sultry smile. "Trouble? People say that's my middle name."

"You are trouble." His lips barely moved. His eyes were harder than the diamonds that graced Fliss's neck. "I don't want you talking to Savvas. Leave him alone. You're not getting your talons into my brother."

Her defiance wavered. Damon's brutal reaction was predictable. Before she'd met him, she'd heard tales about him.

Of his business successes, his clever, decisive mind, his devastating good looks. But she'd never expected the raw, primal emotion he'd aroused in her. They'd met at a wedding she and Fliss had organised for a business colleague of his. She'd taken one look at the gorgeous guy with the dark, brooding magnetism and fallen. Hard.

He'd been charming, attentive, interested—she'd thought. Until he'd learned her name, figured out that she was Aaron Grainger's scandalous widow. In an instant he'd changed. Withdrawn. Become distant and, worse, disinterested. She'd watched his eyes narrow, and with one raking glance he'd stripped her to the soul, then he'd dismissed her and stepped past her to congratulate the groom. But it had been far too late for caution. She'd been lost.

Caught up in her thoughts, Rebecca let her hips move fluidly to the rhythm of the music. For a moment his body responded and they moved as one, dipping and swaying. But an instant later he tensed and moved away.

Always it had been so.

After that first encounter, she'd searched him out shamelessly, using business acquaintances and her connections as Aaron Grainger's widow to secure invitations to places he frequented, inexorably driven by a raw attraction that had gone to the heart of her. How hard she'd tried to recapture that magical moment. Always she imagined a moment of softening, a flash of heat, then it was gone—and the man of steel returned. Until finally she'd realised the overwhelming attraction existed only in her own mind.

Damon hadn't seemed to feel anything.

The discovery crushed her.

Even now, as they danced, his body was rigid, unbending, his gaze fixed on something over her shoulder. Totally removed from her. Her mouth twisted. So much for fate. Nothing in her life had ever been easy, so why should falling in love be any different?

But she'd *never* expected fate's final cruel twist: that Damon would take one look at Fliss's sweet blond gentleness and want it for himself. Or how much that would devastate her.

And there was nothing she could do about it.

Last night had proved that.

Oh, God, last night…

She stared at his mouth pressed into a hard line, remembered the hard, seeking pressure against her lips, remembered how…

No, no, don't think about it!

So Rebecca said the first thing that came into her head. "Both you and Savvas dance well. Did you attend lessons?"

"Forget about how well Savvas dances, you little trouble-maker," he ground out. "I want you to stay away from him, he's too young."

Troublemaker?

Why the hell not. What did she have to lose? Rebecca blocked out his disparaging voice and, humming the refrain of the waltz, let her body brush his, heard his breath catch and repeated the fleeting brush of body against body.

"*Theos.* Stop it!" The hand on her waist moved to her shoulder, a manacle, holding her at bay.

She resisted the urge to sag in his arms as despair overwhelmed her. Forced herself not to crumple, to stay tall and straight and move lightly, with grace, on feet that felt leaden. She gave him a mocking little smile. He glared back, more than angry now.

His disgust, his distrust, seared her.

What was she doing? She sagged against him, the struggle going out of her. His body tightened, then firm hands pushed her away, holding her at a distance. The ache inside intensified. What was she trying to prove? Damon was right. *This was wrong.* However much he'd hurt her, however much she felt he deserved her bad behaviour, Fliss's wedding was not the place for it. Nor was it worth losing the only thing she had left—her self-respect.

But there was no reason she shouldn't needle him just a teeny-weeny little bit.

Her spine stiffened. She shot him a swift upward glance. "Savvas told me he's twenty-seven. That's three years older than me. I'd say he's the perfect age for me."

"Listen to me!" Damon sounded at the end of his tether. "My brother is light-years younger in experience. No match for a woman like you."

The words stung.

"A woman like me?"

Anger swirled through her at the injustice of it all.

Damon Asteriades didn't even know what kind of woman she was. How could he be so blind? How *dare* he fail to recognise—*refuse* to recognise—what lay between them? He should not be marrying Fliss today—or any other woman for that matter. Damn him, there was only one woman on earth he should ever have contemplated marrying. *Her*.

There. She'd admitted it.

Admitted what lay at the heart of her pain. What he'd always refused to recognise. And now it was too late.

He was married.

To her best friend.

Yet still this *thing*…this force…burned with a life of its own, bigger than both of them. And sometimes, like now, she almost convinced herself he was aware of it—even feared it. Experimentally Rebecca let her fingers slide along the shoulder of his wedding suit, over the fine fabric of his white shirt collar, until she touched the bare skin of his neck. She thought—dreamed—she detected the smallest of shudders.

"Shame on you! You know nothing about me," she whispered and blew gently into the soft hollow beside his clenched jaw. "You never chose to find out anything about me."

He started. "For God's sake! What's to find out? I know more than I ever wanted." Bitterness spilled from him. "You're a black widow. You grasp and demand and devour and leave nothing behind."

"That's a—"

"Lie? *Is it?* But there's nothing to disprove my words, is there? You married Aaron Grainger for his fortune, and when everything was gone you drove him to suicide."

She gasped. "You know, no one has *ever* dared say that to my face before." Helplessly she flapped the hand that a moment ago had stroked his neck. "I heard the rumours existed, but I never thought anyone of substance believed them. I certainly never thought *you* the type to believe gossip."

The hand on her waist tightened. The tempo of the music quickened. The dancing speeded up, building to the finale.

"Yes, but I've got more than gossip to go on, haven't I? *Haven't I?*" His face was pressed up against hers now. She could see her reflection glittering in his eyes, could smell the heat of his fury. "I know exactly the kind of woman you are. The kind that kisses her best friend's man, begs him to—"

"Shut up!"

He spun her around, pulled her close to avoid another couple. "You promise sin and desire and deliver nothing but carnal delight. I know the temptation you are. Only last night—"

She froze in his arms and came to a sudden jarring halt.

"I said shut up," she huffed. "Or do you want me to cause that scene you're so terrified of? Here, on Fliss's big day?" Standing dead still on the dance floor, no longer able to move, she watched the realisation dawn as he became aware of where they both stood, of what calamity had nearly befallen them, and watched the mantle of iron control drop into place as the next melody began.

"I must be mad," he bit out, his voice full of self-disgust, and he reared back as though he feared she might contaminate him.

The sheer force of his words released Rebecca from the insanity that held her rooted to the ground. If he was mad, then she must be trapped in the same madness.

Damon was married. Untouchable. Better she remember that.
Shrugging out of his arms, she spun around and stalked away.
He let her go.
And she didn't dare look back.

Two

Almost four years later

Tuesday morning started badly. Rebecca overslept, and by the time T.J. managed to wake her, his insistent little fingers squeezing her cheeks, the dazzling almost-summer sun was already well up in the cloudless Northland sky.

T.J. was querulous as she hurriedly dressed him. Guilt took over. Yesterday she'd stayed home, taken him to the doctor for the earache that had plagued him over the weekend. Last night he'd cried a little before finally dropping off to sleep, leaving Rebecca to toss and turn for most of the night listening out for him. But he'd slept through.

Promising herself that she'd cut her workday short and spend the afternoon with him, Rebecca rushed him out the door and strapped him into the car seat, while he grumbled incessantly.

The whole drive over, Rebecca tried telling herself that

Dorothy—T.J.'s caregiver and a former hospice nurse—was far better qualified to look after T.J., that she wasn't deserting her baby when he needed her most. To no avail.

Dorothy, bless her kind heart, took one look at T.J.'s mutinous expression and opened her arms wide, promising he could watch a *Thomas the Tank Engine* DVD so long as he drank some juice and ate sliced mango and apple first. T.J.'s face brightened instantly and Rebecca heaved a giant sigh of relief.

After Rebecca handed over T.J.'s medication, Dorothy fixed her with a sharp glance. "Don't you worry yourself about this young man. He'll be fine. You stayed with him yesterday when he needed you most. Today you can fix your attention on Chocolatique."

The understanding beneath the brisk words made Rebecca's throat tighten.

As if sensing her volatile, emotive state, Dorothy murmured, "Now, now, Rebecca, off with you, and don't forget to bring me those almond truffles I'm so addicted to when you collect our boy."

"Do I ever forget?" Rebecca gave the older woman a fond smile.

The glow of good humour that Dorothy generated stayed with Rebecca all the way to Chocolatique. There, on the threshold of her business, all remnants of pleasure evaporated and she came to a shocked, gut-wrenching halt.

Him.

Damon Asteriades sprawled across the wing armchair nearest the door, showing total disregard for the designer suit that he wore with the casual abandon of the very wealthy. In a flash, Rebecca took in the highly polished handmade leather shoes, the open jacket and loosened tie, incongruous in Tohunga. At this time of year the town was populated by European backpackers in T-shirts, shorts and sandals. Up, up went her eyes over the finely carved mouth…up…until his chilling narrowed gaze propelled her into action.

She crossed the threshold, apprehension parching her mouth, and croaked, "What are *you* doing here?"

"The one good thing I remember about you, Rebecca, was your polish, your semblance of manners. Has living up here in the back-of-the-beyond stripped the last veneer of civilisation from you?"

Rebecca stared into the brutally handsome face, at a total loss for words.

He straightened. "I have a matter I need to discuss with you."

"With me?" Rebecca's heart lurched. What was he doing up here in Tohunga, hundreds of kilometres north of Auckland? Had the day of reckoning, the day she'd been dreading for more than three years, finally arrived?

Damon gestured to the empty chair across from him. "Do you see anyone else?" His dangerous pirate face was unreadable, harder than ever, new lines bracketing his full mouth, but it lacked the killing anger she'd expected.

"What do you want with me?" And immediately wished the tense, hasty words unsaid. Don't panic, she told herself. Keep it calm, polite. Don't let him see the dread.

He didn't answer. Instead his unnerving gaze swept her from head to toe.

"You haven't changed."

It didn't sound like a compliment.

Rebecca knew she shouldn't allow him to rattle her. There was nothing wrong with her appearance. The sundress was well cut and appropriate to the warm October spring morning, her long ebony hair secured in a neat French twist. Unless her emotions gave her away, he would see only a well-groomed woman in total command of herself and her surroundings.

She took her time returning the inspection. The suit would be Italian. Armani perhaps. The unbuttoned jacket revealed a white shirt. It would be made of the finest silk, she remembered, hand tailored for him. Fitting the muscled body beneath to perfection.

Wrenching her gaze away, she stared into cool blue eyes. "So what do you want?" Certainly not her. He'd never wanted her. But T.J.…well, T.J. was another story.

Rebecca swallowed the bitter, coppery taste of pure terror.

Chocolatique was *her* business, she reminded herself, coming closer.

And *he* was the interloper.

Yet Chocolatique, with its familiar comforting fragrance of chocolate, the warm red and amber tones of the cosy, elegant decor she had spent days selecting, failed to dispel Rebecca's fear.

Vaguely she registered that the shop was humming. With the exception of the one empty armchair opposite Damon, every seat in the shop was taken. Even the booths, carefully divided by screens and lush palms in pots to maximise privacy, were full. Yet the rise and fall of busy chatter failed to muffle Rebecca's unwanted awareness of the man who watched her as though he expected her to turn tail and run.

Oblivious to the tension, Miranda, her assistant, smiled a greeting from behind the spotless glass counter where dozens of delicacies containing chocolate in some form or another were displayed on hand-painted ceramic platters. It was still too early for the busloads of tourists who stopped in on their route to Cape Reinga for refreshments and to sample and purchase the delicately decorated chocolates several local women produced. For the sake of her regular customers who came each morning for cups of rich chocolate or mochaccino, Rebecca forced a smile.

"Rebecca…"

The rich, rough velvet of his voice caused tingles to vibrate up her spine. She shivered as every muscle in her body tightened. How did he do it? One word, and she reacted like a cat to its master's touch.

But she was no pet.

She was a woman. Her own woman. Damon Asteriades no

longer held any power over her. She no longer fancied herself
in love with him. So she flashed him a careless smile. With
deliberation, she folded her arms across the high back of the
empty armchair opposite him, determined to show herself—
him—that he had no longer had any effect on her. "Good
morning, Damon. I would recommend—"

"I am done." He cut her off, and the newspaper across his
knee rustled as he set it aside and leaned across the coffee table
toward her. From her vantage point Rebecca couldn't help
noticing the thickness of his silky black hair, the breadth of
his shoulders under the fine fabric of his superbly fitting suit.

Then his fingers brushed hers and she gave a tiny, breathless gasp.

Before she could snatch her fingers away, he slid a rectan-
gular piece of paper into her hand. Automatically she took it,
then glanced down.

Instant déjà vu.

It was a cheque issued from a premier account, the bold
gold print signifying that the bank deemed the signatory to
be of great importance. Closer investigation revealed an
obscene number of zeros, an amount far in excess of—she
glanced at the empty coffee cup and crumbs and smudges that
were all that remained of a slice of chocolate cheesecake—
what he'd ordered.

"You appear to have overpaid," she said drily.

"For breakfast? Perhaps."

"For whatever," she retorted, his confident, lazy tone
making her hackles rise. But she couldn't stop herself from
glancing back at the plate in front of him. Chocolate cheesecake for *breakfast?* Her mouth twitched. But then, Damon had
always had a sweet tooth.

"Ah, but that is not payment for 'whatever' as you so col-
loquially put it."

His words wiped away all residue of humour. Something
in the way he watched her, the unwavering concentration,

caused blood to rush to her face and her heart to start hammering. His full, gorgeous mouth twisted, and she tensed.

"No. The cheque is not for services rendered. At least not the kind that you clearly have in mind, *koukla*, if your flushed cheeks and bright eyes are anything to go by. Avaricious women never were much of a turn-on for me."

Humiliation scorched her. The worst of it was the knowledge that his words held more than a grain of truth. Clever, astute Damon had read the hope that had flooded her as her heart thudded—the hope that for once he'd experienced the same intense, hot flaring awareness she had.

Naturally the coldhearted bastard didn't feel a thing, while she trembled from the aftershock of the raw want that blasted through her, leaving her nipples tight and her body weak.

Damn him to the fires of hell.

She wasn't going to cower behind an armchair, she decided. She wasn't scared of Damon Asteriades. Nor did she fear the effect he had on her. That was nothing more than lust. Her heart was safe.

Stepping around the chair, she thrust the cheque back at him. "Take this and shove it!"

She told herself she could withstand his powerful magnetism. Because lust without love meant nothing—except bitter emptiness.

Instead of taking the cheque and ripping it up, he laid it very deliberately, faceup, on the small round table between them in a gesture loaded with challenge. "Now the negotiations start." He gave her a hard smile, but his glittering eyes held no humour. "Don't forget—I know that women like you are always on the lookout for easy money, for a wealthy benefactor."

Oh, how the barb hurt. "Get out of Chocolatique," she whispered, her lips tight. "I am not for sale. Ever."

He stared at her without blinking, then said very calmly, "You are overreacting. Whatever made you assume I'd *want* to buy you?"

How could she ever have loved this man? Believed that he might learn to love her back if he only knew her? Beyond speech, Rebecca glared at him, anger chopping through her, churning in her stomach. His gaze dropped and her breath caught in her throat.

The formfitting sundress splashed with red-and-white hibiscus flowers on a black background had seemed such a good idea earlier this morning, cool in the humid Northland climate. Yet now she felt exposed, naked. She refused to fold her arms and hide the puckered nipples that still pressed against the cotton fabric.

Her body switched treacherously to slow burn as those eyes traced the curve of her breasts, then lowered to the indent at her waist, making her feel like some concubine on the auction block. Except there was nothing sexual in his carefully calculated assessment.

Damon was putting her down, she told herself fiercely. This was his way of underscoring the fact that while she still desired him beyond reason, he detested her absolutely. She spun away and retreated so the high back of the empty armchair once again formed a solid barrier between them.

Had anyone else noticed the humiliating interaction? A glance toward the counter showed that Miranda was handing a customer a large box of truffles tied with a red organza bow, while one of the full-time waitresses Rebecca employed carried a tray laden with steaming cups and muffins to a secluded booth on the other side of the shop. No, she concluded, no one in the room was aware of how she felt—no one except Damon.

Resentment and desire smelted together, twisting tighter and tighter inside her until she wanted nothing more than to swing around and let rip and rage at him. But she refused to grant him that satisfaction. She would far rather see *him* flip, lose all control and go up in flames.

Her lips pursed at the wishful image. Little chance of that

happening. Damon was a total control freak. But she needed to find out what he wanted, what had brought him and his chequebook here. And the best way to find out was to provoke him. Carefully.

She swivelled to face him. "So what are you doing in Tohunga?" And raised an inquiring eyebrow. "Slumming?"

With some satisfaction, Rebecca heard the impatient breath he blew out.

"You are not going to get under my skin, woman. I promised my mother…"

"Promised your mother what?" She pounced on his words, the fear she'd refused to recognise easing.

He gave her a resentful look. "My mother, for some reason, holds you in high regard."

"I've always liked her, too. Soula has style, good taste and isn't as prejudiced as some." And she smiled demurely as fury flashed in his vivid blue eyes.

Through gritted teeth he said, "Savvas is to be married. My mother wants you to arrange the wedding."

"I'm sorry, I don't do weddings anymore," Rebecca replied without a hint of apology, her confidence returning at his bald request.

The blue eyes spat sparks and an almost-forgotten exhilaration filled her. For the first time since she'd known him she had the upper hand, and she relished it.

"No, you don't plan elaborate occasions anymore, you run a little sweetshop." He made it sound as if she'd come down in the world.

Rebecca ignored the taunt. "Did Soula tell you that she called me a fortnight ago to ask me to do the wedding?"

He inclined his head a small degree.

"And I told her that I had a business to tend, the 'little sweetshop', as so you quaintly put it. I can't up and leave— even if I wanted to." By the curl of her lip she hoped he got the message that she intended to do nothing of the sort. Never again would she put herself in Damon's range. "I'm sure your mother is more than capable of putting together and organising a wedding. She's a resourceful woman."

"Things are not as you remember. My mother..."

"What?" Rebecca prompted, something in his lowered voice, his taut expression, causing unease to curl inside her. She let go of the back of the armchair that she'd been clutching onto for support and stepped forward into the secluded circle that the seating created.

He hesitated. "My mother suffered a heart attack."

"When? Is she all right?"

Damon's face hardened. "The urgency of your concern does you credit—even if it is two years too late."

"Two years? I didn't know!"

"And why should you?" A red flush of anger flared across his outrageously angled cheekbones. "You are not among our family's intimates. I never wanted to see you, speak to you, again. You got what you wanted. You destroyed—"

He broke off and looked away.

Anguish slashed at her. Rebecca bit her lip to stop the hasty, impetuous words of explanation from escaping. "Damon..." she murmured at last.

He turned back, and Rebecca looked into the impassive, tightly controlled face of a stranger.

"*Then pirazi.*" He shrugged. "What the hell does it matter? The past is gone." He spoke in a flat, final tone from which all emotion had been leached. "All that counts is the present. My mother thinks arranging the wedding will be too much for her, given the state of her health."

"Why doesn't the bride's family assist?"

"Demetra came out on a visit from Greece and met Savvas here. She doesn't have the contacts—nor the inclination—to organise a function of this magnitude. As for her family—they live in Greece and will be flying out to New Zealand shortly before the celebrations, by which time it will be far too late."

Rebecca met his eyes. The restless force that lay behind the Aegean-blue irises still tugged at her.

Oh, God.

How could he still have this effect on her? Hadn't she learned a thing in the past four years? Apparently not. But she knew that to give in to his demand would be folly. The risks were too high.

She shook her head. "I'm sorry…"

His eyes sparked again. "Spare me the polite niceties. You're not sorry at all! But consider this—I'll make it well worth your while, pay you more than that." He gestured to the cheque on the table. "Then you can get someone in to run your little sweetshop."

He was throwing cash at her. Rebecca wanted to laugh in his face. Money didn't motivate her, whatever Damon thought.

"I don't think you could pay me enough to—"

"No need to bank my cheques any longer? Got another rich fool at your beck and call?"

The fury was back in full force.

This time Rebecca did laugh.

Damon bulleted to his feet and grasped her shoulders. "Damn you!"

His aftershave surrounded her, hauntingly familiar, a spicy mix of lemon and heat, mingling with the sexy scent of his skin. Then, just as suddenly as he had grabbed her, he dropped his hands from her shoulders as if he couldn't bear to touch her and swore softly, a string of Greek words, the meaning evident from his intensity. "I must be mad."

Resentment smouldered in his eyes as he sank back into the armchair and raked both hands through his rumpled hair.

And suddenly all the triumph Rebecca had expected to feel fell flat. She gave a quick glance around the shop. Still they had excited no attention. Unnerved by the powerful undercurrents swirling between them, Rebecca plopped into the armchair opposite him.

Hidden now by the high wingback armchair and the shielding palms in tall urns, she felt as if they'd been transported to another world that contained just the two of them…and the uncomfortable tension that lay like a tangled thread between them.

Damon sat forward, breathing hard. "Rebecca, my mother needs your help. I am asking you, *please?*"

He hated begging—she could see it in the tight whiteness of his clenched fists. Strangely she didn't enjoy seeing him in this position. She imagined Soula's strength diluted by physical weakness, knew what it must have taken the proud woman to ask for help a second time.

Then she thought of T.J., of everything that could go wrong.

There was no choice. "Damon…I…I can't."

"Can't?" Now the contempt was palpable. "Won't, I think. I don't remember you being vindictive, Rebecca. Strange, because I thought that in this cat-and-mouse game between us vengeance was *my* move."

Her heart stopped at the brooding darkness that shadowed his face. "Is that a threat? Because if it is, you can go," she said, her voice low, her spine stiff. "And when you leave, please don't slam the door behind you. Now get out."

There was a long, tense silence.

Damon didn't move.

Rebecca's nerves screamed with tension as she held his fathomless gaze. When she decided she'd finally gone too far, speaking to wealthy, powerful Damon Asteriades as though he were nothing but a hooligan, he spoke at last.

"Is that my cue to say 'Make me'?" he asked gently, then leaned back in *her* armchair in *her* shop.

If she hadn't known better, she'd have thought him completely at ease. The act was so good, in fact, that when his gaze swept from her face, over her body, down the length of her legs, discomfiture followed.

"You couldn't evict me—even if you wanted to," he continued, his gaze minutely examining her slim frame.

"Oh, for heaven's sake, stop playing games, Damon." Weariness infused Rebecca, followed quickly by impatience. "And lay off the long, lingering looks. I'm aware that you wouldn't want me if I was the last woman on Earth—"

"If you were the last woman on Earth, I'd say the men remaining would face a fate worse than death."

"Oh…" Her growl of frustration made him give that cold smile she hated. She loved seeing him laugh properly, his teeth flashing white against his tanned skin, revealing the sensual curve of his mouth. But this travesty of a smile never touched his watchful eyes.

"You'll have to learn to master that short fuse one of these days, Rebecca. Your eyes are flashing, your cheeks are scarlet. Again. At a guess, I'd say you're angry enough to…bite."

A further flush of heat swept her at his soft, suggestive words. "Bite?" she retorted. "Ha, you should be so lucky."

The smile stretched, revealing even white teeth. "I have no idea what any man would see in you. You are a vixen, a hellcat."

At least that made a change from the tired old labels of "black widow," "money-grubber"…

"Of course you wouldn't recognise my worth! You go for passive women you can dominate, force your will on."

"We will leave Felicity out of this." His voice was icy, his smile gone.

She widened her eyes. "Now why would you assume I was speaking of Fliss? She finally found the courage to stand up to you, to do what *she* wanted—"

"Be quiet." The whisper was a warning.

But Rebecca paid no heed. "No, I'm referring to the women you've been seeing for the past two years. Dolls, all of them."

"Ah, Rebecca, you disappoint me! You've been reading cheap gossip rags. I can assure you, the magazines got it wrong. They are not dolls," he purred, his mouth softening in a way that revealed masculine satisfaction and made her hands ball into fists.

"You're right, they're not even dolls. They're no more than cardboard cutouts. All identical. Skinny and blond and—"

"Jealous, Rebecca?"

Anguish exploded within her. Beyond thought, she drew back her right arm. His cool, narrowed gaze acted like a dash of freezing water and halted her intention to land the blow.

Coming rapidly to her senses, Rebecca peered around the edge of the armchair. Still no one watching. Thank God. Peace of mind, serenity and respect had been hard-earned in this small town. She wasn't going to let them be ripped away by one tempestuous public outburst.

Grimacing, she turned back to glare at him. "One day…" she muttered.

"You're not the first person to contemplate my untimely demise with great pleasure," he drawled.

She stared at him, shaken by the shock wave that went through her at the thought of a world without him in it. Reluctant to examine the implications of that realization, she hurriedly stood and scooped up his empty plate and cup and saucer with shaking hands.

He was on his feet instantly. "Retreating, Rebecca?"

I have to. But she remained mute, averting her face.

The sudden grasp on her elbow was firm but not painful. "Sit."

"No." She shook off his hold, frantically blinking away the sting of anger and hurt that she refused to let him see. Before she'd realised his intent, he'd taken the crockery from her hands and set it back on the table.

"Sit," he said again.

"I can't." She met his gaze, determined to appear cool and composed. "I've got work to do, orders to courier out." It wasn't a lie. Chocolatique was a successful operation. In addition to tourists who stopped to taste and buy, she had plenty of customers in Auckland who regularly ordered boxes of handmade chocolates by e-mail and phone.

"Rebecca, I am a busy man." He sank back into the

armchair, crossing his ankle over his knee. The cuffs of his fine silk shirt shot back, and he glanced impatiently at the Rolex on his wrist. "Right now I should be in Auckland finalising a sensitive business deal, not cooling my heels here. But my mother's health and happiness are more important than anything else in the world. So I ask you one final time to reconsider your position—it will be worth your while."

Despite his obvious impatience, his tone had changed, the offensiveness now gone, his jaw tight and his lean body coiled and utterly still as he waited for her reply.

It maddened Rebecca that he still thought he had only to wave a leather-bound chequebook and she'd fall into line. Like everyone else did. But not her. Tossing her head back, she gave him a withering look. "You've used that line to death, Damon. Four years ago you offered me money to stay away from Fliss—"

"But you couldn't, could you?" he growled. "Couldn't bear for her to find happiness, not when you wanted her man."

"No!" She covered her ears. "I'm not listening to this."

He came out of the armchair like a spring unwinding, fast and furious. Grabbing her wrists, he thrust her hands away from her ears. "Yes, admit it, Rebecca. Six weeks you let her have. Six weeks before you enticed her away. You were desperate for—"

"No," she repeated more loudly now that the offensiveness was back in full force. She glared at him. "It wasn't like that."

He bent toward her until his nose almost touched hers and his glittering blue eyes filled her vision. "God knows how you convinced Fliss to go with you in the end."

Perhaps the time had come to stop worrying about his reaction and to tell him the bald, tragic truth. That should stop him in his tracks.

She drew a deep, shuddering breath, and courage came in a rush. "She came of her own accord. I didn't force her. I told Fliss about my b—"

"Stop! I don't want to hear your lies. You stole my wife after only six weeks of marriage, and that is something I will never forgive! I will not listen to your lies." Damon was breathing hard, his eyes dark with anger. "But for you, my wife would still be alive."

He released her abruptly and she reeled away, realising with shock and horror that whatever she told him, he was not going to believe a word she said. She closed her mouth, rubbing her wrist absently. Rebecca heard his breath catch and his hand shot out.

"Let me see." The fingers that closed around her wrist were gentle. There was silence. She stood still, tense under his touch as his thumb massaged the spot where he'd held her. Then he said tonelessly, "I am sorry."

Rebecca stared at his long, tanned fingers resting against her wrist. "It's okay. There's not even a mark."

His voice rose. "It is *not* okay. I hurt you." Her head shot up. His beautiful full lips were drawn in a tight line, white and bloodless.

Rebecca bit back a hysterical giggle. He'd hurt her far worse in the past by refusing to believe in her integrity. He hadn't even liked her. *That* had hurt. Withdrawing her arm from his grasp, she smiled sadly. "You didn't—and it doesn't matter. Really."

His eyes were a brilliant, unfathomable blue. "So what do you say, Rebecca? Arrange Savvas's wedding and let's put the past behind us. Call it quits, hmm?"

She flicked him a glance.

Damon was prepared to bury the old resentments and bad feelings—perhaps there was a chance they could reach a truce. So that one day she would be able to tell him about T.J. And then there was that other temptation…

If she helped with the wedding—not for payment, of course, she couldn't do that—but to achieve a truce—then Damon might get to know her, might even discover what she'd always known, that they were bound by invisible ties too powerful to ignore. But…

Doubt assailed her.

Damon was a wealthy, powerful man. What if he found out the truth about T.J.? She simply couldn't risk T.J.'s security to chase a pitiful fantasy that she might—might—change Damon's poor opinion of her.

She sighed. "Look, I told you—I don't do weddings any more." Defeat weighed her down. Whatever she'd once felt for him he'd trampled into the dust, making it clear that he despised her. She waved a dismissive hand at the cheque on the table. "Not even for that ridiculously large amount of money."

"But my mother—"

"Your mother knows I can't do the wedding. I told her myself!" Soula had sounded fine on the telephone two weeks ago and the heart attack had taken place two years ago. This helpless sense of letting Soula down was just Damon's manipulation. In his world the end always justified the means. "If you want, I'll call her and tell her again that I can't do it."

Alarm lit his eyes. "I don't want you—"

"Talking to your mother. I know, I know!" Because he didn't want her finding out that he'd lied about his mother's health? Or because he didn't want Rebecca Grainger, a woman he utterly despised, having anything to do with his beloved mother?

He tried to say something, but she held up a hand, a new burn of hurt searing her at his appallingly low opinion of her, until all she wanted to do was hit back. "So please tell her not to call me again. And I don't want you bothering me, either. My answer stands."

His mouth snapped shut, an uncompromising line in that hard, wildly handsome face, while his eyes glittered with menace.

Yes, it was past time she accepted that there was nothing that she could salvage from the past, nothing that would make Damon look at her through kinder eyes.

"Now, you say you're such a busy, important man—you'd better get back to Auckland."

Rebecca didn't wait for his reply. One last reproachful look, then she whirled and bolted through her shop, ignoring the turning heads, until she reached the safety of her rabbit hole of an office behind the large workmanlike kitchen, shaken to the core by their bitter exchange.

Hours after their confrontation, Damon strode across the forecourt of the chain hotel of which he'd just checked out. Long shadows cast by the row of cypress trees edging the boundary crept like dark fingers across the cobbled pavers, reminding Damon that the afternoon was waning.

Had he heeded Rebecca's parting shot this morning, he'd already have been back in Auckland, closing the Rangiwhau deal. The CEO had demanded a face-to-face meeting this afternoon. Damon had stalled. Instead of concluding a lucrative deal that would make his shareholders a killing, he'd spent the afternoon closeted in a hotel room, juggling conference calls, working like a demon…all the while plotting how to get Rebecca to change her mind. And trying to rid himself of the ridiculous notion that he'd wounded her.

Impossible. The woman ate men for breakfast.

Damon had a fleeting memory of Aaron Grainger.

A good man. A shrewd banker who'd advanced Damon a hefty, much-needed loan in the nightmarish period after his father's death. Ari Asteriades had believed himself invincible. He'd made no provision for key personnel insurance, left no liquid funds available. Because of Aaron, Damon had managed to fight off the circling sharks and save Stellar International, keeping control in the family, keeping his tattered pride intact.

Aaron Grainger certainly hadn't deserved to die broken and bankrupt. Damon had heard the tales about Rebecca's profligacy. The fabulous designer wardrobe she'd ordered after her honeymoon, the jewels she'd demanded, the expensive flutters at the bookies on the racecourse, the overseas trips she'd insisted on. How she'd convinced a besotted Aaron to support her impulsive business schemes, all of which had demanded huge resources.

And then there had been the story about her lover. A handsome drug addict she'd begged Aaron to bail out of trouble. Rumour had it that Aaron had put his foot down that time. The lover had been history—but only after Aaron had paid off his horrendous debts.

Damon's jaw tightened. Reaching the Mercedes, Damon opened the trunk and tossed in his overnight bag and laptop case. Aaron should have put a stop to it sooner, before his beautiful wife had driven him to death—and dishonour.

No doubt about it, Rebecca deserved whatever she got.

He slammed the driver's door harder than he'd intended and stuck the key in the ignition. The ring of his cell phone interrupted his angry musings, and he jabbed a button on the cell phone where he'd just secured it against the dashboard. "Yes?" he demanded.

"Will she do it?" Savvas asked.

There was no need to ask to whom Savvas was referring. Reluctant to report his failure, Damon responded, "How is Mama?"

"Feeling dizzy again. The doctor is concerned about her. He says she worries too much, that she must take things easy."

"Or?" Damon knew there had to be a consequence. Dr. Campbell was not given to fussing unnecessarily.

"Or she could have another heart attack, and this time…" Savvas's voice trailed away.

"And this time it might prove fatal," Damon finished grimly.

"Don't talk like that!"

"It's the reality." Damon could almost see his brother crossing himself superstitiously at his words.

"You know, Damon, sometimes I wish I'd never asked Demetra to marry me. This damn wedding—"

"This from the man who preaches true love?" Damon cut in mockingly, disturbed more than he cared to admit by the idea that Savvas might be having second thoughts.

"No, no. I don't mean that I would forgo having met Demetra or falling in love with her. She's the best thing that ever happened to me. I meant I should have moved her in with me."

"*Vre*, the family would never have stood for it. Thea Iphegenia would've fainted in horror."

"Yet they turn a blind eye to the women you escort, Damon. They don't accuse you of sinning." Savvas's complaint filled the car's interior.

"That's different. I'm a widower. And anyway, I choose women of the world, not maidens with *marriage* written all over them, like your Demetra," he told his brother, his mouth twisting. He stared unseeingly through the windscreen into the golden glow of the late Northland afternoon. Felicity had been his last foray into respectability. It would be a cold day in hell before he tried it again.

"Maybe it would've been better to marry in court, present Mama and the family with a fait accompli. But now it's too late—the big Greek wedding is already in production. Damon, I fear it might kill Mama."

"Savvas, Mama wants this wedding. Desperately. Can you deprive her of it?"

His mother asked for so little. And gave them so much. Instead of retreating into tears and grief after his father's unexpected and devastating death, she had battled beside him as he'd wrestled for control of Stellar International. She deserved happiness, contentment.

Stupidly he'd thought his marriage would secure that.

He twisted the key. The Mercedes roared to life.

"Mama says she wants to hold a grandchild in her arms before she dies," Savvas was saying. "Demetra wants to start trying for a family as soon as the honeymoon's over. But first we need to arrange the wedding."

His mother lived for her family. *Family looked out for family.* That was his mother's creed. Cold, bitter rage twisted inside Damon's heart. All his mother wanted was to see Savvas wed. Rebecca could pull it off. Easily.

But Rebecca had already refused his mother's direct request—and now she'd refused him. He wasn't a man accustomed to refusal. Rebecca *would* help his mother and organise his brother's wedding. He'd make sure of it.

With slow deliberation he put the gear into reverse.

"It cannot be easy asking *her* for help. You hate her. I mean, not that I blame you or anything." Savvas faltered, then sighed. "Look, there's something I must tell you. After the wedding I saw her a couple of times and she seemed…quiet. I didn't see anything of the wild, wicked woman people talk about—"

"Hang on, are you telling me you *dated* Rebecca while I was on my honeymoon?" The car idled. Damon felt an almost forgotten red tide of rage boil up within him. *Hell.* He'd told her to stay away from Savvas.

"She's a very beautiful woman." His brother sounded sheepish.

"Beautiful?" Damon snorted. "If you like black widows. She's as dangerous as sin to the unwary."

"But, Damon, she wasn't like that!" Then, after a taut pause, Savvas amended hastily, "At least I could've sworn she wasn't like that. She was kind to me. We had some good times."

Good times? He didn't like that one little bit. Damon found he didn't even want to contemplate the implications. Reversing the car out of the parking bay in one smooth manoeuvre, he swung the steering wheel and headed smoothly for the exit. "No, of course she wasn't *like that*," Damon said bitingly. "That's her game. She spins her web, and the victim steps in."

There was a long silence. "Well, it's past." Savvas sighed more heavily this time. "After what she did, I didn't contact her again. You're my brother—how could I?"

Inside the suddenly silent Mercedes, Damon was fiercely

glad that Savvas had proved loyal to him and hoped it had cut Rebecca to the quick when Savvas had failed to call her again.

Savvas was speaking again and Damon forced himself to concentrate. "To see her, it must be hard for you. If she comes back to Auckland, it's going to cost—"

Damon cut him short. "Whatever the cost, I will do it. For Mama."

He clicked off the phone and swung the Mercedes into the main street of Tohunga. This time he'd do what he should've done from the outset: use charm. Rebecca had never made any bones about the attraction he'd held for her in the past. A little flirting, add a couple of handsome cheques and she'd be putty in his hands.

The empty parking space right outside Chocolatique gave him considerable satisfaction. It was all working out. As he entered Rebecca's shop, Damon straightened his tie, squared his shoulders and pasted a breathtaking smile to his face— one that guaranteed women would fall at his feet.

But Rebecca was not there. Gone for the day, he was advised by her blushing assistant, who kept sneaking him little looks from under her lashes.

Five minutes later, his smile gone, seething with impatience, Damon gunned his Mercedes down the road to Rebecca's home, determined to be out of this parochial town within an hour. And equally determined that when he left, Rebecca would be sitting beside him—whether she liked it or not.

Whatever the cost.

Three

Rebecca nosed the little yellow hatchback into the drive of the neat compact unit that had been her home since she'd sold Dream Occasions almost four years ago and relocated north.

In the small front garden the cheerful daffodils had finished flowering. The petunias and calendulas she and T.J. had planted were starting to bud. Soon the garden would be awash with colour and summer would be here in full swing. A large pohutukawa tree shaded the grassy spot where she and T.J. often played during the day. By the time Christmas came the massive tree would be covered with showers of flame-red flowers.

She switched the engine off and, turning, saw that T.J. had fallen asleep cradled in the car seat in the rear. His dark curly head drooped sideways and his mouth parted in an O.

Tenderness expanded inside her until she felt she would explode with emotion.

How dearly she loved him.

They were a family. No, more than family. In a relatively short time he'd become her whole world. All her reservations about what a poor mother she'd make given her lack of loving example had long since evaporated. She loved T.J. with all the fierce adoration of a lioness. He was hers. All hers. For once in her life she had someone that nothing and no one could take from her. Today she'd kept her silent promise and had rushed through her tasks at Chocolatique to spend some quality time with T.J. this afternoon. Except for dark shadows beneath his eyes, little sign remained of yesterday's illness.

With a still-sleeping T.J. bundled in her arms, Rebecca made for the unit, her stride quickening under his leaden weight. As she stepped onto the deck, a tall man straightened from where he'd been leaning against the wisteria-covered pergola that shaded the deck. Rebecca froze.

"You have a child!" Damon's voice was accusing, his face blank with shock.

Her grip on T.J. tightened. "Yes," she bit out and, radiating defiance, she faced him down over T.J.'s head.

A muscle worked in Damon's jaw. He looked odd, shaken. She frowned. If he suspected…

No. It wasn't possible. She'd taken such care.

She swivelled away, keeping T.J. screened from his line of sight.

Damon stepped out of the shadows formed by the tangle of ivy and wisteria. "I didn't know."

"And why should you? I don't count you among my intimates."

His head snapped back as she parroted his response from this morning back at him, and Rebecca watched over her shoulder with feline satisfaction as his pupils flared at her sharp tone.

Good! Let him know what rejection felt like.

Her gaze swept the street. "I don't see your car." The sleek silver Mercedes would've been difficult to miss in the empty street.

"I parked around the corner."

"Oh?" Had he suspected she might run if she knew he was lying in wait for her? Had he already known about T.J.? Was this a trap? But then, why play out the shocked charade pretending that he didn't know the child existed? Thoughts whipped back and forth until her head started to ache.

"T.J. hasn't been well. He needs rest. So you'll have to excuse me." Rebecca hitched T.J. higher, measuring the distance to her front door, anxious to escape.

"Wait a minute." Before she could reach the wooden door, Damon barred the entrance and took the keys from her nerveless fingers.

"What's the matter with him? And what the hell kind of name is T.J.?"

"What's wrong with T.J. need not concern you."

Ignoring the second part of the question, she shouldered her way past Damon and made for the carpeted stairs, determined to evade him. But the sound of his footsteps hard at her heels told her she'd failed.

Rebecca halted in the doorway of T.J.'s bedroom, keeping her back firmly to Damon. "You don't need to come in. You can wait downstairs."

He ignored the obstruction she'd attempted to create and stepped past her, his gaze roaming the room, taking in the sunny yellow walls, the mound of soft toys at the foot of the bed, the wooden tracks and brightly coloured trains in the corner.

The room shrank, Damon's powerful presence reducing it to the size of a closet. Rebecca was uncomfortably aware of his unwelcome proximity…of her rapid, shallow breathing.

Why couldn't he have stayed downstairs? And why did her body still respond to him with such irrational intensity? Rebecca ground her teeth with frustration. "Look, T.J. needs his sleep. The last thing I want is for him to awaken and find some strange man in his room."

Damon swung his attention away from the train-station mural she'd painted in bold colours on the wall above the bed, his gaze clashing with hers, his sensuous mouth askew with mockery. "He's not accustomed to waking to find strange men in his house? Now that amazes me, Rebecca."

The inference took her breath away.

"Now listen to me," she huffed. "I don't give a f…fluff what you think of me. But in my house, around my son, you will address me with respect. Right now I'm tired and T.J.'s been unwell. I need to put him to bed."

All at once the tension that had been throbbing inside her became too much. She bit her lip and looked away, blinking furiously, determined not to let the unaccustomed prick of tears show.

"I'm sorry."

For some reason, his unexpected apology was the last straw. Her throat thickened unbearably. She swallowed and shot him a desperate look. "Please…"

"Just go?" he finished, giving her a strange, whimsical smile, and crossing to the bed, he pulled the *Thomas the Tank Engine* cover back. "That's not the first time I've heard that today."

She moved closer, T.J. heavy as a block of lead in her arms. "Then I'm sorry to bore you," she said in a thin, high voice that sounded totally foreign compared to her usual husky tones.

"Bore me?" His mouth dropped open, his eyes glinting with something she didn't quite recognise. *"Bore me?"*

The sudden silence rang in her ears. Damon was standing so close she was conscious of his height, of the solid breadth of him. If she stretched her hand out around T.J.'s sleeping body, she could touch Damon's chest, feel the strong, vibrant beat of his heart.

"I think boring is one thing you could never be guilty of, Rebecca." He blew out hard, muttered something softly in Greek, then said with a touch of roughness, "Here, let me take the boy."

She jerked away as his fingers brushed her arm.

At once, the hands reaching for T.J. pulled back and

Damon spread his palms. "Okay, okay, I get the message! I'll wait downstairs." He threw her a hard, glittering look. "Never give an inch, never show any weakness, hmm?"

Rebecca ducked her head, refusing to meet his angry eyes, reluctant to reveal how much the electrical charge of the accidental touch had unnerved her. After a moment Damon's footsteps retreated, and for a wild instant she felt a sudden stupid sense of loss. Shaking, she hugged T.J. tightly against her breasts and inhaled his special baby smell until her turmoil calmed.

Then she gently deposited T.J. onto the royal-blue sheet and held her breath as he rolled over and gave a short grunt. He didn't waken. Instead his breathing steadied into the deep rhythm of sleep.

For a minute Rebecca stared at his sleeping face, the soft baby skin, the tousled dark curls, and pride and love stretched her heart to a tender pain.

T.J.

T.J. was her priority now.

Not her career. Not Damon. Not the wild, all-consuming attraction that had once upon a time nearly destroyed her. The most important thing in her life was T.J. And he rewarded her devotion with an uncritical, unconditional love that she would never, ever consider trading for the ferocious and destructive passion Damon had once stirred.

Damon's narrowed gaze and the sheer, untrammelled intensity emanating from him as he stood legs apart, arms folded, caused Rebecca's nerve endings to prickle warningly as she entered the living room.

"The boy is sleeping, yes?"

"Yes," she replied, pausing inside the doorway, more unsettled by his speculative stare than she cared to admit. Her gaze slid away. Took in the tailored suit that accentuated the hard, sleek lines of his body. His trademark white silk shirt was open at the neck, tie gone, the top button undone to reveal a glimpse of his tanned throat. She yanked her gaze back up to his face.

"I'm sorry he is not well. Is it something serious?"

The genuine concern in those devastating eyes forced Rebecca to say, "Just a routine ear infection."

He frowned. "I understand ear infections can be dangerous—that they can lead to permanent hearing loss."

Damon was vocalising her worst fears. Only yesterday she'd expressed the very same concerns to T.J.'s doctor—not that she'd ever admit that to Damon. Instead she tossed her head and said casually, "The doctor assured me a course of antibiotics will do the trick."

"So where is the child's father?"

The indolent question fell like a heavy rock into a tranquil pool, destroying any pretense of neutrality.

Rebecca stiffened.

"No longer in my life," she said, deliberately vague, avoiding the blue eyes that she was certain would be blazing with disapproval. The pause that followed stretched until her palms started to sweat. Fighting the urge to steal a fleeting glance at him, she kept her gaze lowered, uneasy with the turn the conversation had taken.

"Do you even *know* who his father is?"

Her head shot up, her affronted gaze colliding with his, and all at once she was too angry to fret about what she might give away. "What the hell kind of question is that? Of course I know who T.J.'s father is!"

She forced her expression into impassivity. Keep your cool, she counselled herself and then said aloud, "This is my home. I'd thank you to keep your…observations…to yourself. Now what can I do for you?"

"I ask no more than that you arrange Savvas's wedding," he replied, echoing her studied civility.

"I've already told you—I can't!"

"Rebecca," he said through gritted teeth, the false courtesy vanishing, his face darkening. "You know I'm a very wealthy man—"

Rolling her eyes, she interrupted him. "I already told you this morning I can't do the wedding and I'm not going to accept payment. You've done the bribery and corruption thing to death. Cutting the insults would be a good move, too." She held her breath and waited for him to explode.

His eyes flashed. His chest rose and fell under his crossed arms as he sucked in a deep breath. Then he sighed heavily. Unfolding his arms, he spread them wide. "Okay, whatever it takes to get you to do this damned wedding thing, I'll do it. So I can get back to Auckland and put my mother's mind at rest."

Rebecca blinked, stunned by his sudden capitulation. Damon did not negotiate, he issued ultimatums—and expected them to be met. A fresh wave of guilt rolled over her. Soula had always been kind to her. But helping Soula with the wedding was out of the question.

"What? No clever comeback?" Damon stared at her, his jaw clenched.

All at once, Rebecca recognised the truth of what he'd just said. Years ago, when they first met, she might have reacted to his statement that he'd do whatever it took with a risqué taunt like *Kiss me and I might consider it*. Comments that had drawn derision, followed by a closed, cold expression that shut her out. Totally.

Contrarily, it had been his very lack of response that had egged her on, demanding his attention by whatever means she could. And then had come the dawning realisation that he was interested in Fliss. While Rebecca burned anything she touched, Fliss cooked like a dream—a legacy of her Cordon Bleu training—and Damon had savoured rich slices of Sachertorte with half-closed eyes, his face alive with pleasure. Her heart breaking, Rebecca had watched him smile at Fliss with warm approval, his face reflecting an intent admiration he'd never shown toward her. Pretty, sweet Fliss, who was as different from Rebecca as a rabbit from a lioness.

Rebecca had backed off, waiting for Fliss to spurn him. But she hadn't. Fliss had had no right—

Stupid! Why did she keep getting tangled in the web of the past? She shook her head wildly, trying to dislodge the memories that still tortured her. No. That was all old history. Fliss was dead.

Instantly the urge to provoke Damon withered. Inside she felt flat and empty, worn out by the toll the emotional day had taken.

"Don't shake your head. Think about it. You can use the money for your business…for the boy." His gaze roved pointedly around the room, highlighting the tired carpets that needed replacing, the lounge suite that was showing signs of wear. "Surely money won't come amiss in jazzing up your lifestyle in this dull town. I can't see why you stay."

Rebecca stared expressionlessly at him. Going back to Auckland would simply reopen the old wounds. But for a lingering instant she considered the cheque Damon had dangled in front of her this morning. Now he was making it clear that the sky was the limit.

She *couldn't* accept payment to arrange Savvas's wedding. It wouldn't be right.

But, said a little evil, tempting voice at the back of her head, what might it mean to T.J.?

Although Chocolatique made them a fair living, it was a relatively new business that demanded time and all her resources. And, yes, she had a reasonable lump sum squirreled away in T.J.'s name that she intended to release to him on his twenty-fifth birthday. But what Damon was offering would eliminate years of worrying….

No! Rebecca thrust the temptation away. She couldn't accept his money, not for arranging an exclusive Auckland wedding. And she certainly had no intention of being in Damon's debt. Ever.

"My place is here," she said firmly. "I have T.J. to look after."

Damon looked flummoxed. It was obvious he hadn't factored a child into his calculations. But the confusion that clouded his brilliant blue eyes cleared almost immediately. "No problem. Bring the boy, too."

Rebecca laughed, a light, tinkling social laugh that carefully hid the sudden tightening around her heart. Bring T.J.? That was the last thing in the world she wanted!

"Get real, Damon. What would a child do in the Asteriades household? Destroy the antiques? Wreck the formal borders in the garden?"

Damon stared down his battered nose at her. "Demetra happens to like children. I'm sure she'll give you a hand if you ask nicely."

Demetra? His obvious fondness for the woman struck a raw nerve.

"And exactly who is Demetra?"

"I told you." He sounded impatient. "She is Savvas's fiancée."

"I'd forgotten her name was Demetra." Rebecca tried to ignore the relief that scalded her. And then annoyance kicked in. What did it matter who Damon's latest lover was?

Damon gave her a level stare. "Demetra is perfect for Savvas. She's kind, respectable, well brought up…."

Everything she wasn't. Each word landed like a well-placed barb. Recklessness flooded Rebecca. "Does she know what she's letting herself in for, marrying into the Asteriades clan?" she lashed out. "At least she's clever enough to realise what a bigot you are and how much nicer Savvas is."

"Ah, and you would know, wouldn't you?" He drilled her with narrowed, bitter eyes. "Savvas told me that the two of you dated after the wedding. How…*nice*—" he sneered "— were you to my brother, hmm?"

She flashed a wide white smile that didn't reveal any of the mix of emotions churning within her.

Anger.

Excitement.

And the thrill of danger that sparring with Damon always brought.

Softly, provocatively, she said, "You warned me to stay away from him, but Savvas called, said he wanted to see me. Your little brother liked me for myself. After the way you'd humiliated me, that was...*nice*." Staring through her eyelashes at him, she held her breath and waited for his response to the pointed mockery.

He didn't disappoint her.

His eyes flared brighter. "You little tramp..." He stepped abruptly closer. "You slept with my brother to get revenge on me. Because I married your best friend!"

Pain blossomed, but Rebecca refused to let him intimidate her. "Perhaps you place too much importance on yourself, your effect on the behaviour of others. Savvas lacks your arrogance—another reason why he is worth a million of you."

"Your mouth drips poison." He stalked closer still, his eyes blazing. "But I will deal with that."

The air had become electric, pulsing. Rebecca stood her ground. "Why the double standard? You can insult me with impunity, but when I retaliate..."

After a humming moment that pulsed with old resentments, latent attraction and myriad unspoken emotions, Damon spun on his heel, strode across the worn carpet and dropped down onto the homely sofa. For a long moment Rebecca stared at large, tanned hands clenching and unclenching between his thighs. Hands that could touch with the softness of silk or the cruelty of steel. Hands that made her shiver...and burn.

She forced her gaze back to his masklike face. He'd withdrawn. How she hated that.

"Forget it. I am not coming to Auckland." Rebecca spoke with finality, and when a sense of calm filled her, she knew she had made the right decision.

Turning away so she didn't need to see his expression when he realised that he had failed his mother, she closed off her mind to guilt. Damon had a dangerous effect on her. He aroused such reckless cravings she dared not risk being close to him.

"Look, I'm sorry."

She jumped as he spoke behind her; she hadn't heard him rise, or cross the room. She swung around. A dark lock had fallen onto his forehead. He brushed it back and sighed. More guilt stirred when she took in the unaccustomed tiredness in his eyes, the deep lines scored beside his mouth.

"I don't know what came over me. I swore I wouldn't let—" he shot her a hooded glance "—what happened in the past affect my dealings with you. I meant to be amenable." He flashed her a smile that might've been described as irresistible if it hadn't been directed at her.

Rebecca's mind started to click over. "You intended—" her breath caught "—to be *nice* to me."

His eyes flickered and a dull, red flush spread across his high cheekbones.

Bingo! Fury rose within her. "How far were you prepared to go, damn you?"

"Wait." He drew a breath. "Right now Mama is my only concern. She needs—"

She cut across before he could defend himself with clever words. "So you would've done *anything*," she said in a bitter little voice. "Used charm, seduced silly Rebecca?"

"No," he burst out. "I wouldn't have taken it that far."

Of course not. Sleeping with her was beneath the powerful, oh-so-perfect Damon Asteriades. "Well, fortunately for you it won't be necessary to go to such extremes. I can give you the name of someone who will plan a wonderful wedding for Savvas. Two someones, in fact. I'm sure the sisters who bought Dream Occasions would love the chance—"

"No!" The look he gave her burned with frustration. "I tried all that, but Mama insists on you. She trusts you and she's too on edge for me to risk arguing with her." He raked long fingers through his hair, but the recalcitrant locks fell forward again, dispelling the powerful-billionaire image.

Rebecca closed her mind to his boyish vulnerability and focused instead on the fact that Damon had tried to argue Soula out of asking for her help, on the fact that he truly seemed to believe his mother couldn't cope.

The trap was closing around her.

"Please help Mama. The child won't be a problem," he was saying. "We can work something out."

He was desperate.

As much as she wanted to slap him, punish him, Rebecca felt increasingly guilty that she had refused. Soula must be very unwell for him to go to such extremes. But how *could* she help? She had to put T.J.—and herself—first.

He's seen T.J., a little evil voice whispered. *He hasn't put it together.*

Dared she risk it? Rebecca chewed her bottom lip, thinking furiously. "It's not only a case of T.J. What will happen to my business while I'm away?"

Sensing her weakening, his blue eyes sharpened. "Surely your business can survive your absence for a couple of weeks? Later on, a lot of the wedding arrangements could be made from here. The move to Auckland won't be permanent."

"I don't know…." For a thread of time she wavered, and then all her misgivings crashed back. *What would happen if the truth came out?*

"Look, I'll double the amount of that cheque I offered this morn—" The jangle of Damon's cell phone caused him to break off.

The interruption made her hiss with relief. What was she thinking? She was mad even to consider it. Nothing, not even obscene amounts of money, would make her go back.

* * *

Almost. He'd almost had her!

Damon snarled a string of curses in Greek as he checked the caller ID. At the familiar number, a cold frisson ran down his spine and he stopped cursing abruptly. He rose, tension coiling in his gut, and stalked away from Rebecca, toward the blankness of the dark window.

"Mama? What is it?"

"Damon, I've been having pains in my chest. Savvas and Demetra are taking me to the hospital."

"Has Savvas called the doctor?"

"He's meeting us at the hospital. He says I'm going to have to stay there for a couple of days. My son, what am I to do?"

"Rest," Damon responded succinctly and stared out the window into the darkening night. Through the gloom he could barely make out the shape of the large tree rustling in the front garden.

"But what about the wedding? What about—"

"Don't give it another thought. I've got it all under control." Over his shoulder he shot the stubborn, maddening woman on the other side of the room a smouldering glance.

"Rebecca's going to do it? Oh, that's wonderful! I can't tell you how much peace of mind that brings me! Bring her to the hospital—I need to tell her what I've done, who I've spoken to, the venues I've considered."

He couldn't admit to his mother that he had failed. She had to believe he'd succeeded. For the sake of her heart. He'd handle what he'd tell her when he arrived back in Auckland, without Rebecca, later. Damon wondered for the thousandth time why his mother was so fixated on Rebecca. The women who had bought Dream Occasions from Rebecca would have leaped at the chance to arrange an Asteriades wedding.

It burned him that out of all the women in the world, his mother had to choose the one who had killed his marriage. Yet his mother refused to accept that Rebecca was to blame—

had always insisted that Fliss must have left of her own accord. Damon didn't—couldn't—accept that. But how could he refute it? He'd never told anyone, least of all his mother, about what had happened on the eve of his wedding….

All he could do now was murmur, "I will bring her. Hush now. I want you to relax. Do not worry about anything, I will take care of everything."

Rebecca found herself holding her breath as she listened to the one-sided conversation. With every sentence Damon's cheekbones stood out more starkly under tightly stretched skin, his tan draining to an unflattering putty shade.

Something twisted deep inside her as those rough fingers raked back the dark spikes of hair that had fallen forward over his eyes. And when he stared so helplessly into the night, his shoulders hunched, she had to force herself to be still, not to rush to his side, not to rest her hand on his arm, touch him…anything to banish the stark shock and bewilderment as he uttered frantic words of comfort.

"Mama? Mama…" He now called with desperation. "Can you hear me?" A shaking hand jabbed through his hair. "No, no, don't answer. Just get to the hospital. I will meet you there."

He ended the call and turned to Rebecca, his eyes dark sunken pits in his bleak face.

"I have to go back to Auckland. My mother—" He wheeled away, placing a fisted hand against his temple.

Rebecca felt terrible. He hadn't lied. All the time he'd wasted trying to convince her, time he should have spent in Auckland, near his mother.

What if Soula died? What if Damon didn't make it in time, never saw his mother again?

She would never forgive herself! And if Soula died, who would take the hurt from Damon's eyes? Damon always looked after his family—who would be there for him?

Full of remorse, she hurried toward him and touched his sleeve. He started. "Damon, I'll come with you. I'll take care of…of…Savvas's wedding."

At the back of her mind lurked the awful thought that if Soula died, there would be no wedding, at least not until the mourning period was over. *Please,* Rebecca prayed, *please let Soula live to celebrate a wedding.*

The Asteriades mansion hadn't changed one iota, Rebecca saw as Damon swept into the formal curved driveway four hours later. The beam from the headlights illuminated neatly trimmed box hedges and large pots planted with bay trees that flanked the front door.

Back in Tohunga, a frantic rush had ensued before they'd left. In a matter of minutes Rebecca had made several necessarily brief phone calls. Miranda—with the help of her sister—would take care of Chocolatique until Rebecca returned. A call to her doctor assured her that T.J. was fit to travel, so all that was left was for Rebecca to arrange for the local handyman to mow her lawn and to pack.

During the journey Damon had made countless calls to Savvas and the doctors to check on his mother's progress. And although Savvas had repeatedly assured him that Soula was in good hands, that the heart attack had been arrested, under Damon's tightly leashed control Rebecca sensed his terror. That he might lose Soula, as he had already lost his father.

Oh, God, how well she understood his fear of loss. For once in his life Damon faced something he couldn't control. And she had no defence against his anguish. She could no more turn her back on him than she could cut off her arm.

Now, facing the imposing Georgian-style facade that loomed against the night sky, Rebecca shivered. It wasn't only Auckland's cooler night air that caused the ripples of gooseflesh. This house held memories she desperately wanted to forget. For a short time Fliss had lived here with Damon.

Even the elderly man who removed her suitcases from the trunk was familiar. Johnny, Damon's live-in butler.

"This way."

Rebecca turned at Damon's voice. T.J. was slung across his shoulder, fast asleep. She rushed over. "I'll take him. You go to the hospital."

But Damon carried on up the wide stairs lit by brass lamps to the front door. "Never fear, mama bear, I won't drop your baby. I'll show you your rooms, then I will go to the hospital. Savvas says Mama is sleeping peacefully."

Inside, Rebecca saw that the passage of time had wrought changes. She halted and stared with confusion at the three corridors that led from the spacious double-height lobby with its pale, glossy marble floor. Ahead, she recognised the stairs that led to Soula's rooms, but the red carpet had been pulled out and replaced with pale wool carpeting in an elegant oyster shade.

"I converted the wing Savvas and I shared on the ground floor into a suite of rooms for my mother after her heart attack. It made things easier—she didn't have to worry about the stairs."

That strong streak of protectiveness, Rebecca recognised. Damon took care of his own.

He headed for the staircase. "Demetra is staying in Mama's suite until the wedding."

Her heart fluttering, Rebecca asked, "And T.J. and me? Where will we be staying?"

"In my quarters."

Rebecca faltered. "Your quarters?"

Ahead of her, Damon paused on a landing. "Savvas and I had Mama's old suite extended and refurbished. But now Savvas has moved out—he bought a house where he and Demetra will live after the wedding—so it is mine alone."

Rebecca forced herself to follow him down a well-lit corridor glassed from floor to ceiling on the left. Through vast sheets of glass she could see a darkened courtyard where the flat gleam of water glittered blackly below.

He caught her sideways glance. "I replaced the old pool. The new one is more practical."

She remembered the fussy, elaborate pool with pockets of frothing water connected by artificial waterfalls and fountains decorated with fawning statues. A previous owner had possessed terrible taste. "You swim laps?"

"Every morning."

Rebecca made a mental note to keep away at that time. Then she thought of T.J.'s fascination with water. "Is the pool fenced?"

"The only access is through the house—and a gate in the garden which stays locked. I will give instructions to the staff to secure the ranch sliders at all times."

"Thank you."

"This will be your room." He opened a door to a room decorated in restful shades of cream. Curtains of heavy damask complemented a bedcover fashioned of rich ivory silk. On the wall hung a Monet print—or it might even be an original—the pale water lilies drifting on a pond adding to the restful mood of the room.

"And T.J.? Where will he sleep?"

"Through here."

She followed Damon into the adjoining room. It was smaller, clearly intended to be a dressing room, but a bed had been set up with bright, crisp new linen, while a selection of brand-new toys crowded the floor.

She pulled back the covers and he lowered T.J. so gently that her baby didn't even sigh. Deciding that T.J. could sleep in his clothes on this one occasion, Rebecca pulled his sandals off and fussed with the covers.

"There are bigger rooms, but I thought you would want the boy near you."

"Thank you." His thoughtfulness surprised her. Her gaze lingered on the array of toys. "But you didn't need to go to so much trouble—or expense."

"There wasn't much time. Johnny had a little over an hour

before the stores closed this evening. But I wanted your son to be settled, happy, while you are in Auckland. I don't want you fretting. If a few toys make the adjustment a little easier, then so be it." He gave a shrug.

Rebecca's heart contracted. That shrug—it was so intrinsically Damon.

She straightened, desperate to escape the sudden claustrophobia that cocooned them in the small, cosy room. Rapidly she made her way across the bigger bedroom to the large curtained windows. Pulling the heavy drapes aside, she stared out into the night.

In the courtyard below, the long, narrow pool mirrored the ripe moon, and through the open side windows Rebecca detected the scent of orange blossom and a whiff of jasmine on the night air.

"I need to go to the hospital. I'll leave you to settle in." Damon's voice sounded husky.

"Thank you."

But she heard no sound of footsteps, no thud of the door shutting behind him.

Driven by curiosity, she turned. He was watching her, an unreadable expression on his dark pirate face. The intense blue eyes were full of shadows, caused by the anxiety and concern for his mother, no doubt. But despite his uncharacteristic vulnerability she could still feel the pull that he'd always exerted.

She swung back to the window and stared blindly out, her back as tense as steel wire, her pulse hammering.

"It is too dark now to see how much better the courtyard looks with the lap pool and the landscaping I had done." His voice was low.

She wished he'd leave. Before she made a fool of herself. All over again.

"You always had a good eye," she admitted, her spine stiff. Old memories stirred. He'd picked out the wedding dress he'd wanted Fliss to wear. It had been perfect, enhancing her prettiness to almost become beauty—a far cry from the girlish flounces Fliss would have chosen.

"I'm honoured that you recognise my redeeming qualities." Irony tinged his voice.

Rebecca didn't respond.

A rough sigh came from behind her. "Again I must apologise. That was not necessary. You agreed to come, to help my mother with this infernal wedding that has her so worked up for some reason. Enough, it appears, to put her in hospital. The least I can do is extend true Greek hospitality."

"It's all right, Damon." She spoke to her faint reflection in the dark window. "I don't expect anything from you. Your feelings for me have always been plain."

He shifted behind her. "Have I been that bad?"

Rebecca drew a quivering breath, fortifying herself against the almost playful note in his voice. The last thing she needed was Damon extending false friendship because he felt obligated. Where would that leave her?

Head over heels in love?

God, no! Honest dislike was far, far better than false hopes.

"No reply? Not what I'd expect from you, Rebecca. What are you thinking, standing there so silent?"

That was a first. Damon had never been interested in her views, her thoughts. Too often he'd stifled her opinions with a harsh look, his mouth drawn into a sneer.

"Lost for words, hmm?" Again that hint of playfulness. "Or too polite to tell me that you think I've been worse than I suggest?"

She lifted a negligent shoulder and dropped it, refusing to be drawn…or charmed.

The silence stretched. She inhaled and became sharply aware of the heady fragrance of the orange blossom—and her awareness of the man behind her soared. She heard the soft rustle of silk as he shifted, heard the tempo of his breathing change. The tension started to wind tighter until Rebecca could stand it no longer and swung around.

He was standing much closer than she'd anticipated. The thick carpet must have muffled his approach. And there was something in his eyes—something elemental, something that she recognised.

Her heart leaped, and speeded to a gallop.

The air sizzled, charged. Rebecca wanted to fling her arms around him, pull him to her, feel his lips on hers. She tried to remember all the reasons it would be a bad idea.

He hated her. He was overwrought, worried by his mother's collapse. He'd been her best friend's husband.

It would be dangerous to T.J.—heck, it would be dangerous for *her*. There was no chance of a happy ending. Only heartbreak would come from this.

Yet none of it mattered. She didn't care. About any of it.

If only he would touch her. Kiss her. Set her on fire.

And when he moved, she closed the rest of the space between them. Breathing his name, she met his gaze, saw the flare of emotion, felt his response leap through her.

Then, as she stretched out her hand and her fingertips touched the firm muscle of his upper arm, he cursed, loudly, violently, and reeled away. But not before she'd glimpsed confusion in his eyes.

A stark, tormented uncertainty.

Rebecca held her breath as he stumbled to the door, and she did not release it until the door slammed shut behind him louder than a crack of thunder.

Four

Damn her!

Damon stepped up to the pool's edge. It was late, well past midnight. But he was too charged to sleep. Rebecca. The child. And the worry of visiting his mother in hospital and demanding answers from the physician on duty. All the events of the day had knotted the tension so tight that now his head threatened to explode. The water lay like a sheet of blackened silver under the moonlight. A moist sea breeze swept his torso and whispered across his thighs but failed to cool the heat that coursed through his naked body.

Upstairs, when Rebecca had tilted up her face, breathed his name…he'd almost drowned in the spell of her beauty. Then she'd touched him….

Tingles bolted through him as he recalled how her electrifying sensuality had wrapped around him. He stared into the flat water and decided she was definitely a witch.

A beautiful, seductive-as-sin witch.

And an avaricious one. For all her talk that she didn't do

weddings anymore, couldn't leave her business, in those moments before his mother called, money *had* finally swayed Rebecca, negating her lofty claim that she was immune to bribery. He snorted in disgust, the sound rupturing the silence of the night.

He was now committed to paying *double* what he'd planned. But what did it matter? The relief that flooded his mother's face at the news that Rebecca was in Auckland made it worth every dollar Rebecca was going screw out of him. Worth even the temporary loss of his own equanimity.

Damon launched himself into space and hit the dark water in a perfect arc, cutting through the silken chill with barely a splash. He surfaced halfway down the length of the black pool and started the long strokes to take him to the other end. Yet, instead of subsiding with each pull of his arms, the seething heat inside him grew.

He should never have asked her to come back.

Rebecca was trouble.

Years ago, from the first time he'd sensed her black, gleaming eyes on him and turned to see her glowing face, incandescent with desire, his interest had been snared. Discovering her name—that she was Grainger's widow—he'd known he was cursed.

It would have been so easy to succumb to the temptation in her beckoning eyes. But he would've despised himself. Instead he'd followed the dictates of his brain, turned his back on Rebecca's highly tempting but indisputably tarnished charms and chosen Felicity, never expecting a day's trouble.

Damon executed a tight racing turn and drove his body faster through the water. What foolishness had caused this ravaging attraction to reignite inside him? The child? Had it been the unexpected shock of discovering that wild, outrageous Rebecca had a child? The first time he'd seen her cradling the boy he'd felt hot and tense and…betrayed.

Mother of God! Rebecca must never discover she'd

breached his defences. A gasping breath and he dived down, down, plunging to the depths of the pool, streaking along the bottom, where the moonbeams were dim, to escape the fear that he would get no rest until he held her lush body naked against his.

Through the window Rebecca stared at the dark, churning water, the image of Damon's naked beauty imprinted on her mind. Every arch of muscle, every hollow of his body had been floodlit by the ghostly moon. She closed her eyes to block out the startling, stomach-tightening images. Desire twisted inside her.

No other man had ever affected her in this way.

Not even Aaron, whom she'd loved for his nurturing succour. Aaron, who'd given her the strength and courage to live her dreams, the support and know-how to start Dream Occasions—and later Chocolatique. But he'd never stirred a fraction of the emotion that Damon did merely by existing.

Oh, God.

Her soul recognised something elemental in Damon. Something that until tonight she'd thought wholly unrequited. Until she'd heard his ragged breathing, seen the shocked realisation, the unwanted knowledge in his eyes and known that he felt it, too. In a flash the future was alight with hope. Then he'd turned away, broken the golden thread of awareness that bound them. Leaving her trapped in the fire of desire.

Rebecca slept badly, and by the time she and T.J. came down to breakfast the following morning, Damon was already eating, engrossed in the business section of the morning paper lying open beside him. Clad in Armani corporate armour, his impressive nakedness hidden, he was every inch the powerful, remote billionaire Rebecca all too often scoured the country's top financial magazines to find. No hint remained of the primal, naked man from last night.

She hurtled into speech. "I'm sorry, we overslept. Are we very late?"

"No. I told Johnny to wait until you arrived so that you could have a hot breakfast." Damon's glance was cool, but he flashed a smile at T.J. before returning to his paper.

Suppressing her hurt at his offhand attitude, Rebecca busied herself with stacking two cushions onto a chair and helped T.J. to clamber up before seating herself beside him.

"I don't want to put your staff to any trouble," she said flatly.

Damon's face was wiped clean of all expression when he finally looked up. "Feeding the boy won't be any trouble."

Rebecca noted wryly that he didn't include her in the assessment. Her mouth slanting, she said, "Well, I don't want to be any trouble. A little fruit, sliced apple perhaps, and coffee would be fine for m—"

"The boy will require more sustenance than that," he interrupted.

A humiliating flush heated her cheeks at the rebuke. "Of course I wouldn't expect T.J. to eat only that. But he doesn't need a cooked breakfast either. Fruit and cereal will be fine."

T.J. chose that moment to utter hopefully, "Sc'ambed eggs, Mum? On toast?"

The look Damon gave her spoke volumes.

She ignored it and said firmly to T.J., "*And* apple slices."

"Okay." T.J. gave her a sunny smile, aware of his small victory.

Little monkey! She ruffled his curls. When she looked up, Damon was staring at her, a strange expression on his face. Before she could break the volatile silence, the door burst open and a petite wiry-haired brunette clad in jeans and a floral shirt rushed into the room.

"You must be…Rebecca?" The newcomer's English was accented, overlaid with an American drawl.

With a shock Rebecca realised this had to be Demetra. She'd expected someone more restrained—more obviously

Greek—than the young woman whose freckled, makeup-free face shone with good health. Rebecca smiled at her and got an answering grin. Then Demetra said, "And who is this handsome guy?"

"My son, T.J." Tensely Rebecca waited for the inevitable questions to follow.

None did. Instead Demetra bolted around the table and sank down beside T.J. "What do you like doing most in the whole wide world?"

"Playing trains." T.J. gave her a euphoric smile and started making *chuff-chuff* sounds.

"Uh, I don't know that much about trains, but I betcha I'll learn. I like digging in the garden more than anything else in the world."

"I like digging in the garden, also. But I like trains more." Demetra laughed. "You'll have to help me dig sometime. What kind of trains do you like?"

"Thomas and Gordon are bestest—they're blue."

"And blue is your favourite colour, right?"

T.J. nodded.

"You'll have to introduce me to Thomas and Gordon right after you've had breakfast. For now, I'll go chase Jane up."

"Jane?" Rebecca queried.

"Damon's chef. She comes in daily and cooks like a dream. Wait until you try—"

"Sc'ambled eggs?" T.J. interrupted worriedly.

"You want scrambled eggs, honey?"

T.J. nodded emphatically. "An' toast."

"Done!"

Demetra rose and was already halfway to the door when Damon called her back. "Better ask Jane for some apple slices for the boy, as well," he said drily. "And Rebecca would like coffee with her fruit."

"Okay."

Then she was gone.

Rebecca blinked. That vital, vivacious creature was Demetra? Her heart lifted. She could see exactly why Savvas had fallen for her verve and warmth. She smiled at Damon—the first real smile since he'd erupted back into her life. "Demetra seems very nice."

"Nice?" Damon raised an eyebrow. "How you like that word."

Rebecca coloured and decided to ignore him. She stayed silent until Demetra returned at whirlwind speed, her arms piled high with plates for herself, Rebecca and T.J.

By the time T.J. licked the last morsel of scrambled egg off his spoon, Rebecca was ready to explode at Damon's rudeness. He'd barely uttered a word, answering only when spoken to and leaving the conversation to herself and Demetra to carry. Not that it had been a hardship; Demetra was a delight. Already she'd offered to look after T.J. while Rebecca visited Soula in hospital later in the morning. Demetra had also confided sotto voce that she viewed the approaching wedding with dread.

"Big, splashy functions are not me. But Savvas says his family expects it—and I know mine will, too, once they get here. So I'm relying on you, Rebecca, to make it a wonderful occasion for the parents. I don't need to know about the choices you make. All I want to see beforehand is the final venue you choose and I'd like to help choose the cake and I want your advice with my dress. Nothing too grand. The rest is up to you!"

"I'll do my best to make it a wedding that you and Savvas will enjoy, as well," Rebecca said, bemused by Demetra's quicksilver personality.

"All I want is Savvas—I love him!" Sincerity radiated from Demetra, and Rebecca wished she'd been blessed with the same love that Demetra shared with Savvas. "Okay," Demetra said more loudly. "Enough of this bride stuff, I'm off for a quick workout in the downstairs gym." And she vanished out the door.

A silence descended in her wake.

Rebecca started to segment the orange she had peeled, an orange she was already too full to eat. She placed two pieces in front of T.J., who attacked them with relish, juice dribbling down his chin.

With a brooding glance in T.J.'s direction, Damon said, "The boy may be excused if he wants."

"T.J. His name is T.J.," Rebecca said impatiently.

"It's a ridiculous name, for God's sake."

"It's his name," she rebuked, dropping her voice. "And he can be excused after he's finished the orange—I'll take him up with me."

Damon leaned back, his eyes narrowing. "What I call him, it upsets you?"

He hadn't taken her advice about Fliss's name preferences on board, so she shrugged. "He's a person, an individual with a name chosen just for him. He's not 'the boy.'"

She put another two segments on T.J.'s plate. He shoved one into his mouth with sticky fingers and picked up the remaining sliver. With a tiny-toothed grin at her, he slid from the chair before she could stop him and was around the table in a trice.

Rebecca watched, frozen, as T.J. offered Damon his last segment of orange. There was a moment of utter silence, then T.J. pushed the messy bit of orange at Damon, insistent now. Rebecca unfroze and leaped to her feet, hurrying toward them, aware that any moment the juice would land on Damon's expensive suit, aware that Damon was not accustomed to three-year-olds and sticky hands and that T.J. was likely to suffer the consequences of his impatience.

Damon's next act stunned her.

Taking the orange, he popped the sodden mass into his mouth. Then he gave T.J. a beaming smile. "Delicious, thank you, T.J."

T.J. squealed with pleasure. He battered his juice-stained fists against Damon's trousers and cackled, "Dee'icious, dee'icious."

Rebecca swept him up into her arms before he could do any more damage. Taking in the wet patches on Damon's thighs with a harassed glance, she said, "I'm so sorry."

Damon shrugged. "No matter. The suit will clean."

He was still smiling at T.J., and Rebecca went utterly still, staring at him. When his head turned, she tore her gaze away. "Excuse us, please." Without waiting for a response, she snatched a paper napkin from the table, flashed him a meaningless smile and made for the door.

"I'll collect you to visit my mother at noon. Be ready." Damon's command followed them out the room.

As she bolted through the doorway, T.J. reached over her shoulder to wave at Damon before whispering in her ear, "I like the man."

It was a shock to see Soula lying so frail and passive in the high hospital bed. Rebecca didn't dare look at Damon. Not that it would've helped. On the drive to the hospital, he'd continued the cold and remote treatment he'd started at breakfast, the silence building a wall of ice between them.

Far better to think about poor Soula, whose chalky pallor was barely distinguishable from the white sheets enveloping her, and whose eyes were closed despite the wide-screen plasma television blaring across a room that looked more like a luxurious hotel suite than a hospital ward.

As the ward door clicked shut, Soula's eyes opened and lit up. "Rebecca, how good to see you! Damon, you're back!" She struggled to sit up, paying scant attention to the drip secured to the back of her hand—or the wiring that protruded from under the bedclothes.

"Mama!" Damon crossed the private ward in two hasty strides. "No, Mama. Lie still."

"Don't be silly. I'm not yet dead, my son. Switch the television off." Damon complied. "Now raise the back of the bed."

While Damon was adjusting the bed-frame setting,

Rebecca approached the high bed, deeply shaken by Damon's mother's appearance. Only the dark, indomitable eyes showed a shred of the proud woman Rebecca remembered.

"I must look a wreck, hmm?"

Rebecca forced a smile, aware that Soula must have read the shock in her eyes but unable for the life of her to think of any platitude that would sound sincere.

"What? No answer, Rebecca?" The older woman gave a wan smile. "Better that than the lies the rest of the family feed me. This morning my eldest sister, Iphigenia, said I still put women of half my age to shame. Pah! All lies!" She rolled her eyes to the ceiling. "But I have to admit it's not as bad as it looks. White is a terrible colour. Look—" she flung an arm out "—white nightdress, white sheets, white blankets. So bad for an older woman—it simply doesn't do a thing for my complexion."

Affection for the acerbic woman overwhelming her, Rebecca bent to plant an impulsive kiss on the cheek that wore a few more wrinkles than it had in the past. "Nonsense," she whispered into Soula's ear. "True beauty comes from within. Hasn't anyone ever told you that?"

They exchanged a long look, then Soula's arms crept around Rebecca's neck and pulled her close. "It's so good to have you here, child. I was starting to despair."

The note of very real desperation in Soula's voice and the unexpected warmth of her hug caused something to splinter deep inside Rebecca and she hugged Soula back fiercely. Swallowing the burgeoning lump in her throat, she glanced up at the bank of equipment above the bed and said in a choked-up voice, "I have to admit I don't like seeing you tied to these machines. When will you be out and about?"

Damon reared up on the other side of the bed, outrage in his eyes. "*Out and about?* My mother needs—"

"Soon!" Soula interrupted her son." I will not stay in this place *ena lepto*—" she held up a thin forefinger "—longer than I need. Not one minute. Look at me! My hair needs attention, my nails need a manicure…." She held out elegant hands spoiled only by chipped nails.

"You should've told me. I would've organised a beautician, a hairdresser—" Damon waved a hand at her nails "—whoever you needed to fix that."

"How can I expect you and Savvas to understand? You are men! Look, I'm wearing nightclothes in the middle of the day. *And* I reek of antibacterial soap." She paused for breath. "I can't bear the smell of the antiseptic."

"Neither can I," said Rebecca with heartfelt fervour. Memories haunted her of the hospital her brother, James, had been in and out of before his death.

Soula gave her a sharp glance. "Only the experiences of the old and sick bring on such strong dislike."

"Perhaps." Rebecca kept her reply noncommittal, aware that she'd already given away more than she'd intended—especially with Damon hovering so close.

Soula patted Rebecca's hand. "One day you will tell me more, *pethi*."

Rebecca looked away. Not likely. It hurt too much.

Every single person she'd loved in her life had been ripped away.

Her parents.

James.

Aaron.

Fliss.

And with Damon she hadn't even got started before it had all come crashing down on her. All she had left was T.J. whom she loved more than life itself.

She blinked. Soula's hand was warm on hers and the weight of it resting there made her feel like the worst kind of fraud.

"Rebecca, *pethi*, I didn't mean to upset you."

Rebecca forced herself to snap out of the black grief that smothered her. Soula should be the focus of her concern now.

"Come, child, let's talk about other things." Soula glanced meaningfully over at her silent son. "Damon, stop glowering and make yourself useful. See if you can find coffee for yourself and Rebecca."

Rebecca winced, waiting for the inevitable explosion to follow the barrage of orders, then relaxed when Damon simply shot her a hooded look, his mouth slanted.

As soon as the two women were alone, Soula patted the bed invitingly, "*Kathiste,* come sit. Tell me what you think about this wedding that has me in such a state."

Not for the first time suspicion rose inside Rebecca and she pinned Soula with a thoughtful look, but the other woman simply smiled and looked angelic.

Raising one speaking eyebrow, Rebecca sat. "And while we talk I'll tend to some of those things that are bothering you so much. Where can I find your vanity case?"

Twenty minutes later Damon padded silently back into the ward. His mother and Rebecca were chatting softly—too softly for him to hear what they were saying—while Rebecca repainted his mother's nails. His mother's crow-black hair had been brushed and secured into a stylish knot that made her look more like her usual immaculate self. Her cheeks held a slight blush, and her lips were coloured with the shade she'd worn as long as he could remember.

Without warning, Soula laughed, and the dull helplessness that had cloaked him since receiving her call started to lift. All at once things seemed brighter. Happier.

His mother was going to be fine. She was not going to die. And he had Rebecca to thank for the transformation. He stepped forward and with his right foot pushed the door shut behind him. The thud caused both women's heads to shoot around.

Rebecca looked instantly wary, but his mother beamed. "Ah, coffee. Rebecca will enjoy that. Won't you, dear?" And without waiting for an answer, she continued. "Put it on the trolley where Rebecca can reach it."

"Two sugars, right?" he asked, unable to help noticing the easy relationship his mother and Rebecca shared. How had he failed to notice the strength of the bond between the two women in the past? Always he'd seen only the differences: one a proud Greek matriarch, widow of one of the richest men in the southern hemisphere, the other born and raised in a series of Auckland foster homes, a woman of questionable morals. One reluctant to succumb to the tyranny of age, the other young and lushly beautiful. Never before had he noticed the common bonds they shared: the strength of will, the burning determination, the stubborn tilt of the chin.

Both were staring at him now, waiting for a response to something he had not heard. He looked from one to the other. "I'm sorry?" he said in his most distant tone, not wanting either woman to conclude that he'd been in dreamland.

"I was commenting on the fact that you remembered that Rebecca takes two teaspoons of sugar in her coffee." For some reason his mother was smiling beatifically at him.

His brows drew together. "She must have told me." But he knew she hadn't. His internal radar had always been attuned to Rebecca's every action. He'd hated it, resented it fiercely. But there hadn't been a thing he could do about it. Except pretend it didn't exist.

And treat her as if she barely existed.

"No, she didn't," his mother said triumphantly. "You remembered from all those years ago."

Backed into a corner, he made the grudging admission. "Perhaps I did."

To his surprise, it was Rebecca who rescued him. "But then, how many women take two spoons of sugar? Not easy to forget. It's something that often makes me self-conscious, my addiction to sugar."

"It shouldn't," he said without thinking. "You can afford to eat whatever you like." And could've kicked himself at her startled expression...and his mother's smug one.

To his relief, his mother didn't comment. Instead she steered the conversation back to Demetra and Savvas's wedding and Damon started to relax.

"I can't help worrying about Demetra. About how she will cope with the strain of a high-profile marriage. She's very..." His mother paused searching for a word.

"Vivacious?" Rebecca inserted with a smile. "But, Soula, that's part of her charm. And don't you worry—as long as Savvas loves her, she'll be fine."

"I hope so." Despite the doubt in the words, his mother looked happier. "But she's not interested in the arrangements at all. The only thing that matters to her is the home Savvas has bought—and more than the house, the garden."

"Some women aren't into the whole wedding spectacle." Rebecca shrugged. "It doesn't mean a thing."

"She has other strengths. She's a landscaper," Damon said.

"Oh, yes, and she's very good with children, too." Soula's eyes lit up. "I can't wait to hold my first grandchild. Damon was very remiss."

Damon felt the explosive reply rising, bit it back and glared at Rebecca. How dare his mother bring this up? To her credit, Rebecca looked extremely uncomfortable.

Even as he glowered, Rebecca rose to her feet. "Speaking of children, I need to get back to the house. T.J. will be wondering where I am."

"I can't wait to meet your son, Rebecca. Does he take after you?"

Rebecca looked flustered. "Not really, although there is some family resemblance. His eyes are just like—" She broke off, blood draining from her face.

Damon took pity on her and said, "He has your dark hair."

"What?" Her face blanked out all emotion. A second later

he watched her snap out of the hell she'd retreated to and reply, "Yes, yes, of course he does."

Damon froze at the undiluted anguish he'd glimpsed in her dark eyes. Eyes so unlike T.J.'s that he concluded that T.J.'s must resemble his father's. A fleeting image of round blue eyes. Again he found himself wondering about the boy's— T.J.'s, he amended—father.

Then he forced himself to dismiss the speculation.

It was not his concern.

Yet there was something about the boy's features that was intensely familiar, but he could not put his finger on what it was. *Then pirazi*—it mattered not. It would come to him.

Rebecca had turned away and was shrugging on her jacket and collecting her bag. Something had stirred up old hurts for her, judging by the speed she made for the door.

"I can't wait to meet the little one," Soula said.

"Soon," Rebecca promised. From the doorway she gave Soula a little wave and bolted.

"You'll have to wait until you get home," Damon said firmly to his mother before kissing her cheek and hurrying after Rebecca.

"Come on, *come on*."

Shifting from foot to foot, Rebecca stabbed the button again, impatient for the elevator to arrive. Hearing Damon's distinctive tread behind her, she shoved her hands into her pockets and hunched into her jacket.

"What's the hurry?" His dark, fluid voice sent shivers that she didn't need down her spine.

"I need to get to T.J. I don't usually leave him for such long stretches of time."

"What about while you work?"

"That's different. He's known Dorothy, his caregiver, since birth. Demetra is a stranger, and the surroundings are alien, too." But even more than getting back to T.J. she wanted to escape. Away from the well-meaning questions, away from Damon and away from the hospital and the memories of awful helplessness it evoked.

An elevator arrived at last, already occupied by a nurse fussing over a hospital gurney. The patient was a young man in his early to mid twenties, Rebecca guessed. One arm was in plaster. What she could see of his face was covered in lacerations, the rest hidden beneath dressings and tape. He looked as though he'd been in a particularly nasty car smash. She stepped inside, transfixed, barely aware of Damon following behind. The patient groaned and turned his head. Rebecca jerked her horrified stare away.

The elevator sank and stopped at another floor. A beeper sounded. The doors slid open again, and the nurse and her patient were gone, the castors rattling against the endless corridor. Rebecca watched the disappearing gurney and prayed fiercely that the young man's prognosis was better than James's had been.

Desperation clawed at her throat. She felt sick, lightheaded. "I need to get out of here."

"It's the hospital, isn't it?"

"I hate these places," Rebecca said with feeling, bile burning the back of her throat.

"Thank you for staying…for helping my mother. It made a great difference."

"It was nothing."

"Hardly nothing. She's afraid." He shot her a searching glance. "Was T.J.'s birth difficult?"

She swallowed hard, disconcerted by the sudden change of subject. His conclusion was not unreasonable in the circumstances. But what to say? "All births are difficult, but the reward is immeasurable. T.J. is a blessing."

"He's a son to be proud of. You've done well, raising him alone."

"Thank you." Her mouth tasted bitter.

If he only knew.

"You had a short stay in hospital after—" He broke off.

"After Fliss died. It was one night." Rebecca kept her tone flat as the elevator jarred to a stop. The doors shuddered open to reveal a well-lit underground car park. Rebecca hurried out.

Damon followed. "Was that when the dislike of hospitals began?"

"It didn't help," she said honestly, stopping and facing him. "But the phobia was already there." James, she couldn't stop thinking of James. The hospitals visits, the hopeless tests, the sudden brutal end. In a sudden blur of pain she remembered the night Fliss died, how she'd cried as Fliss had slipped away. She blinked and forced herself to look up at Damon instead.

His eyes were hooded, but there was none of the tightness in his jaw that she'd half expected. It was the first time Fliss had been mentioned without Damon going up in flames. That had to be progress. Rebecca sighed. She didn't want to fight anymore. She'd had enough.

Seeing Soula weak, ill and older had shaken her. And Rebecca had suddenly been struck by her own mortality. If anything happened to her, what would become of T.J.? She felt a disorientating sense of panic and sagged back against the wall. This was ridiculous! This place must be getting to her. The horrid memories.

Yet deep down she knew it was more than the starkness of the hospital, the haunting memories that called to her from the past. The man standing in front of her—the emotions he aroused—was part of it, too. A sharp ache shot through her head. Dizziness. All at once wide white space closed in on her.

"Hey, are you all right?"

With a sense of shock she became aware of Damon's hands on her shoulders, shaking her gently. For a moment she contemplated leaning forward, resting her head on his chest and releasing the tears she'd held in check for far too long.

But she didn't want to reveal any weakness to him. So she

lifted her head and gave him a wan smile. "I'm fine. Or at least I will be as soon as I get out of this place."

"Let's get you out then."

But he didn't move.

The expression on Rebecca's face caused something to shift in Damon's chest. There was a sadness on the exquisite features, a vulnerability he'd never seen before.

Or had he simply never wanted to see the loneliness?

With a spontaneity that was foreign to him, he leaned forward intending to brush a brief, comforting kiss across her lips. But that all changed the moment his lips touched hers. Instantly he was aware of the softness blooming beneath his. He felt the surprised hiss of her breath against his mouth, and a torrent of desire flooded him.

A primitive male urge rose within him to grind his lips on hers, push her up against the wall, feel her body against his and immerse himself in her heat. To take her and never let her go. Only the confusion in her eyes, the unexpected fragility she'd revealed, halted him.

No.

She had been through enough.

Instead he drew away and cupped her cheek with a gentle hand, heard her breath catch. Her dark eyes were wide and dazed, her lips parted, tempting him. She smelled of flowers, sweet and fragrant. For an instant his mind flashed to that moment in her bedroom when tension and something much more had buzzed between them. That time he'd escaped to the cold, dark water of the pool. But this time…this time he didn't want to stop. Didn't want to be sensible.

He wanted to drop his head, slant his mouth across hers and feel the wildness rock him.

It took everything he had, all his magnificent self-restraint, to leash the passion surging inside him. With careful control he leaned forward and dropped the lightest touch across her nose.

"That tickles." She gave him a small smile and wrinkled her nose at him.

"Does it?" Inside him, something melted. Today he'd seen another, softer side of Rebecca. So very different from the selfish, self-centred woman he'd known before. How patient, loving, she was with her son, how deftly she'd cheered his mother up, easing her fears.

"Yes," she murmured, her lashes fluttering against her cheeks.

A fierce pang of desire pierced him, and he fought to control the need to crush this wild, delicate woman against him. Inexplicably he ached to possess both sides of her—the caring woman and the sexy vamp. He stroked his fingers along her jaw, savouring the soft skin.

Was it the flashes of tender caring that Savvas had seen in her and liked? No doubt her body was another thing his brother had appreciated. Had his brother felt branded by her kisses? The way he did? Damon brooded over the notion and his hand dropped away from her face. Had Rebecca ever aroused this fearful sense of confusion in Savvas?

"Can you stand?" he bit out, then regretted his harshness.

She nodded, visibly pulling herself together, her eyes large liquid pools in her pale face.

Damon stepped back, his reason at war with his body. Fighting the urge to take her into his arms, to surround her with the warmth of his body, to taste her mouth and brand himself with her taste forever. To take her to his bed and keep her there until he discovered every fantasy she craved, stripped away every secret she possessed.

Hell!

His lack of discrimination stunned him. He swung away, disgusted by the insane surge of desire for a woman so many others had possessed. His own brother, Aaron Grainger, other men who watched her salaciously and spoke of her as "hot, hot, hot" and "great in the sack."

"Let's go," he said curtly. "T.J. is waiting."

Then he told himself to stop being stupid. What did he expect? Few women of Rebecca's age had only one lover. Wanting her, bedding her, didn't mean a thing. After all, it wasn't as if wanting equated to marrying the woman.

And he *was* going to have her. *Soon,* Damon vowed bleakly as they crossed the car park, Rebecca silent and withdrawn beside him. It was time to stop fighting the staggering attraction she held for him. And when he'd purged himself, he would walk away, leaving Rebecca and the past behind.

There'd be no loss of control, no emotion.

Only passion.

Five

Rebecca groaned and suppressed the urge to bang her head against the steering wheel at the labouring whine of the car's motor.

What a way to start a Friday morning. For nearly two days she'd successfully avoided Damon, ruthlessly using the wedding as an excuse to spend as much time away from his home as possible. She'd taken advantage of T.J.'s fascination with Demetra—and taken advantage of Demetra's kindhearted offer to babysit T.J.—to get as much organised as she could.

Even though her purpose had been to avoid Damon, Rebecca had been busy. She'd been back to the hospital to check the names of all the guests with Soula and had confirmed late additions with Demetra. A large number would be flying out from Greece, so she'd obtained quotes for their accommodation for Damon to approve. She'd visited the printers, where she'd been given samples of cards, colours and fonts for the embossing on the wedding invitations.

For today she'd lined up appointments to view several

venues for the wedding. But now the battery of the little run-around that Damon had organised for her to drive was flatter than a flopped soufflé. Her fault, of course. She'd failed to close the trunk properly yesterday when she'd returned from the hospital, which meant that the trunk's interior light had been on all night.

She dragged herself out the car and considered her options. Less than ten minutes ago Demetra had waved and driven away with T.J. safely strapped in the back of her sporty little SUV. Demetra planned to take T.J. to feed ducks in a park near her new home. On hearing about the pond, Rebecca had issued a dark warning about T.J.'s fondness of water. Demetra had promised to watch him like a hawk. Afterward she was taking T.J. to her new home for a light lunch and planned to keep him amused planting herbaceous borders in her fledgling garden.

As much as she hated taking advantage of Demetra's sweet nature, she could call and throw herself on Demetra's mercy and beg a ride to town.

Briefly Rebecca considered the other, less appealing option—cancelling her meetings.

"Is there a problem?" The dark velvet voice caused her to stiffen.

Damon.

It would be, of course. After successfully avoiding him, he had to find her beside a car with a flat battery. She'd been rattled by how nearly she'd fallen apart in front of him outside the elevator at the hospital, had intended to be cool, composed, elegant the next time she saw him. More than ever she wanted to kick the capricious car.

Heart sinking, she turned to face him. He looked fantastic in a dark, stylish suit with his usual white shirt and conservative narrow tie below that inscrutable face. Rebecca drew a steadying breath and tried to look more together than the jumble of chaotic emotions inside her allowed. If she told him what was wrong, perhaps he'd lend her another car—Soula's even.

A quick glance at her watch revealed that if she left now, she could still make her first appointment. So she told him. And waited for derisive male condemnation to follow.

"I'll take you," he said abruptly. With a click the electronic-controlled garage door behind her started to rise, revealing his silver Mercedes.

"No, no. That's not necessary."

"Come. Or you will be late." He already had his cell phone in his hand, and Rebecca could hear him instructing his PA to reschedule his appointments and organise someone to recharge Rebecca's car battery as he shepherded her toward the Mercedes.

When he asked where she was going, she told him in a small voice. Rebecca had expected Damon to leave her at the San Lorenzo hotel, but he stayed, striding tight-lipped into the lobby at her side. Rebecca found herself tensing. Of all the places in Auckland, this was the one that held the most painful memories. But it had the grandest ballroom in town. Her own distress was no reason to exclude it from the list of venues.

Andre, a slim, dapper Frenchman who was made for the role of events manager, welcomed Rebecca like a long-lost friend. "You're back in the business?"

With a strained smile Rebecca replied that she was simply doing a favour for a friend. She heard Damon mutter something barely audible about favours being expensive these days. Her brows jerked together in puzzlement. A sideways glance revealed that his mouth was compressed into a hard, tight line.

Rebecca was aware of the precise instant Andre recognised her companion, saw his visible double take. "*Monsieur* Asteriades, it is an honour to have you in our establishment. We are pleased to be of any service we can." The Frenchman quivered like a delighted whippet.

Not for the first time Rebecca's stomach curdled at the ingratiating treatment Damon received wherever he went. He was just a man, for goodness' sake, albeit a gorgeous, sexy man. Andre's deference increased as they walked around the function rooms, the ballroom, until Rebecca wanted to scream.

The tour wasn't made any easier by the gut-churning knowledge that the last time she'd been here had been on the night of Damon's wedding. She couldn't help wondering how often Damon had been here since.

Often, she concluded. What did he care? Of course Damon wouldn't share her despairing memories of the place. He'd only remember Fliss, their wedding.

What the hell did it matter? What she felt about the place was insignificant. Everything had happened nearly four years ago. It no longer had any bearing on the present. Even the decor had changed. Yet the ballroom still retained that rich ambience she remembered, making it the perfect place for a high-society wedding.

"You're not seriously considering this place, are you?" Damon muttered through gritted teeth when Andre whisked away to fetch some sample wine lists.

One look into his stormy eyes and Rebecca knew he hadn't forgotten one minute of that night. She stopped. This was about where she and Damon had parted company after that abortive dance. Even now, a lifetime later, she could recall the burning hurt, the utter misery that had filled her.

But she didn't allow any of the old turmoil to show. Keeping her voice absolutely composed, she said, "It's Auckland's premier venue, the ballroom holds a thousand guests comfortably."

"No."

"No?" She raised an eyebrow at his abrupt refusal, some unkind part of her wanting to make him sweat.

"Absolutely not. While the guests might be comfortable, I most certainly will not." A muscle flexed in his jaw, and his eyes glinted with something that looked like pain.

Perhaps the memory of Fliss, of the happiness they'd

shared that night, was too much? A terrible thought struck her. Had she been wrong all those years ago? Had Damon loved Fliss?

Madly?

Deeply?

Eternally?

And if he had, then he would never accept that she'd simply done what she'd had to the night before his wedding. What she'd believed was right.

"I think you're right," Rebecca conceded, hating the grey tinge that had crept in under his olive tan and hating herself for contributing to it. "It's huge and may be too overwhelming for Demetra. She told me she doesn't want anything too grand."

"Then let's get out of here," Damon said tersely.

Rebecca's second choice of venue was an old, established yacht club that fronted onto the Waitemata Harbour. It was far less imposing, the ballroom more intimate, the view of the water and Auckland's famous Harbour Bridge simply stunning. As the club's function manager guided them around, Damon unclenched his fisted hands and slowly started to relax.

He'd been appalled by the emotion that had smothered him at the San Lorenzo. His towering anger at Rebecca the night of his wedding had come blasting back, an unwelcome reminder of the friction that had existed between them.

Why?

Why had they fought all the time? Why had she insisted on challenging him? Telling him that he couldn't marry Fliss? Provoking him by flaunting her body at him, demanding that he kiss her…and more? And why had he been unable to let the smallest challenge pass?

He could remember wishing Rebecca would behave like Felicity, shy and in awe of him. Felicity had made a lovely bride. But even that memory was tarnished. Somehow he'd failed Felicity. She'd chosen to desert him. Had she known he'd failed her? That he'd betrayed her the night before he spoke his wedding vows?

He'd expected Rebecca to put up a fight against his high-handed veto of the San Lorenzo. Or at least to argue. She'd clearly established a good business relationship with Andre in the past. Yet she'd given in to his demand with barely a murmur. He'd been grateful, silently grateful. How could he, Damon Asteriades, confess that he couldn't bear the idea of celebrating his brother's wedding on the site where his own disastrous marriage had been sealed? Of dancing amidst too many damned ghosts?

Damon told himself he was tagging along to make sure she was fulfilling his mother's brief for the wedding. But he knew it was more than that.

The wanting, the dark desire, had him tied up in knots. And when he'd seen her struggling with the car, the opportunity had been too good to pass up. But he'd also been consumed by curiosity. He'd seen Rebecca the successful chocolate boutique owner, Rebecca the mother and Rebecca the kind friend to an ill older woman. He'd wanted to see more, to see all the facets that made up the enigmatic women who roused such strong responses in him.

As he followed in her wake, Damon had to admit Rebecca was good at what she'd once earned a living doing. Never would he have thought of asking a tenth of the questions listed on her clipboard. Once, she pulled out her cell phone, rang his mother to check whether any wheelchair facilities would be needed and conveyed the negative reply back to their guide. She questioned. She smiled. And each time she laughed, the heat inside Damon grew and he wanted to taste that lush, laughing mouth. *His*. He pushed the disturbing thought aside and watched her jot a note down on a pad. She was focused, professional and totally in charge.

The promise he'd made himself in the hospital car park reared up in his mind. He wanted her. All of her. And there was nothing to stop him having her.

Rebecca finished off, arranging to come back to meet the chef who handled the catering, and Damon reached in his pocket for his car keys. "Well, that's all for now," she told the function manager. "When I return, I will bring the bride to see if the venue fits with her plans."

Rebecca was deep in thought when they returned to the Mercedes. Something bothered her about the yacht club. Something that she couldn't quite put her finger on.

"Time for lunch, I think." Damon's voice interrupted her thoughts.

"Oh, I can't keep you any longer."

"We both need to eat. And there is something I've been wanting to discuss with you. You've been very hard to find, Rebecca, these past couple of days. I might almost think you've been avoiding me."

"Avoiding you?" Her voice was high-pitched. "Why would I do that?"

"If I knew, I wouldn't have had to tag along all morning to get a chance to see you alone."

So he'd stayed because he had an agenda of his own. Rebecca's pulse started to pound. "I don't think—"

"Don't." He held up a hand. "Don't think. Just come and share a meal with me. One of my favourite restaurants is not very far from here. I'll talk. You can listen and savour the food." He gave a slight smile that relieved his usually harsh features.

There'd be more to it than him talking, Rebecca suspected. A frisson slithered down her spine. Yet she was intrigued enough to want to see what kind of establishment he favoured. Even though she knew it was risky. Every minute she spent with him increased the attraction he held. Brought her closer to falling back into the dangerous quagmire of emotions she'd once before barely survived.

Slowly Rebecca nodded her assent.

Not far turned out to be a twenty-minute drive into the country, where Damon finally nosed the Mercedes into a long pohutukawa-lined avenue. The large hand-carved wooden letters against a schist wall announced simply Lakeland Lodge. Through the trees Rebecca caught a glimpse of a large country house and a vast silver sheet of water glittering beyond.

Her breath caught. "How lovely," she breathed.

The lodge radiated serenity. Informal arrangements of country flowers decorated the foyer, and Rebecca paused at a large picture window at the sight of the colourful gardens leading down to the lake.

"What magnificent gardens," she murmured.

Damon smiled. "I thought you'd like it here."

After a moment she took the arm he offered and they made their way to the restaurant, where Damon was greeted with enthusiasm and shown to a table with a fine view of the gardens.

"How on earth did you discover this place?" Rebecca asked after they'd perused the menu and placed their orders.

"In the way one finds out about all best-kept secrets—by word of mouth. I came here to celebrate the silver wedding anniversary of a business acquaintance."

"I never even knew it existed."

"Then I have achieved something. I didn't think there was an establishment in Auckland you didn't know." He gave her a narrow smile. Before Rebecca could retort, their smoked salmon starters arrived and a companionable silence fell between them.

"That was heavenly." She laid her fork down. Taking a deep breath she decided to get whatever he'd brought her here to discuss out of the way. "There is something you wanted to talk about?"

His eyes became serious, intent. His mouth flattened into a grim line. Apprehension flooded Rebecca. She hoped it wasn't what she'd been dreading. Did he suspect…?

Had he worked it out? No, he couldn't have. He'd have given some sign surely. But the gravity of his expression worried her as the seconds dragged past and still he didn't answer.

Just when her nerves reached breaking point, he sighed.

"It's something I don't want to admit. Something I've been fighting for longer than I care to think about."

"What is it?" she asked in a rush.

He didn't reply.

The taut pallor of his face scared her. She pinned on a bright smile. "Come on, fess up. It can't be that bad."

Or could it? Was something wrong with Soula? But, no, she'd spoken to Soula only half an hour ago, and the older woman had sounded upbeat, joking that she would be dancing soon, that certainly she would not need a wheelchair.

Could it be…? Was something wrong with Damon? Horror swept her. She thought wildly of James, of the shock after his diagnosis.

"Are you ill?" She blurted it out and could have kicked herself when his eyes widened.

"No, no. Nothing like that. I want you, Rebecca." He blurted the words out and a blaze of colour stained his angled cheekbones. Her knees went weak at the sight of the naked emotion that flamed in his eyes. Then the controlled mask dropped back into place and she thought she'd hallucinated.

She blinked. Once. Twice. But the remote, powerful businessman remained. Unshakable, hardly the kind of man who would utter such a stark statement with so much haunting desperation.

"What did you say?" she whispered at last as the seconds stretched and the silence grew more strained.

"I want to make love to you." His voice was flat, his face expressionless. He could've been talking about something mundane, something he didn't particularly care much about.

Except she'd seen that hectic, passionate flash of emotion. And a telltale flame of fire still seared his cheeks.

Disbelief floored her. "You can't."

"I'm a man, you're a woman. Why not?" A hint of amusement warmed his eyes, softening his impassive face.

"No." She shook her head wildly.

"Yes."

Spreading her hands apart, she shrugged helplessly. "We can't."

"Why not?" He challenged. "And don't think you can come up with a reason I haven't already thought of and dismissed."

"But—" What was she supposed to say? He'd caught her so off guard she couldn't even think straight. "You don't even *like* me."

He met her eyes levelly. "You're quite right. I didn't think I did."

She flinched, his honesty stinging. "So how can you even contemplate sleeping with me?" There was confusion. Yet somewhere in a deep, hidden part of her, she felt the first hint of rising excitement.

Damon wanted *her*.

"I'm beginning to accept that I must like *something* about you to want you." A ghost of a smile lit his eyes.

Outrage replaced euphoria. "Well, tough! You'll just have to live with the wanting, because nothing is going to happen between us. *It can't*." Did he honestly think she was going to take the scraps that he was throwing to her? Did he think she was that desperate?

Probably.

And he was right. Because she had no pride where Damon Asteriades was concerned. All he had to do was snap his fingers and she came running. Just witness her presence here in Auckland. Witness her presence here in this restaurant today. She'd known it would be a bad idea to spend time with him. But had that stopped her accepting his invitation to lunch?

No. Of course not.

Where Damon Asteriades was concerned, she had the survival instincts of a moth circling a bright flame. But she wasn't ready to be burned alive by him quite yet. No, he was going to have to work a hell of a lot harder. After all, she'd been waiting for him for what seemed like a lifetime. He wasn't going to knock her feet out from under her with a stark statement that he wanted to make love to her. She wanted more. Much, much more.

"Rebecca, stop resisting. I want you and I'm going to have you—the sooner you accept it, the better."

God, but he could be arrogant! "No way. I've been to hell and back because of you before and it's not a place I'm in a hurry to visit again."

He snorted. "You've got that wrong, *koukla. You* almost sent *me* to eternal damnation. You did everything you could to cause upheaval in my life. I meant nothing to you—I don't believe that for a second—it was the challenge that I represented."

You meant everything to me. You were my world, my universe, and you didn't give a damn about me! But she didn't say it aloud.

Instead she shook her head and laughed disbelievingly. "I'm not falling for this."

What was she supposed to say? What was she supposed to think? The man who stirred more emotion within her than she'd known existed *wanted her*. But he fiercely resented the need for her. She'd have to be stupid to take him up on it.

But she was incredibly tempted.

Fool!

Turning him down was going to be the hardest thing she'd ever done. She cast around, struggling to find the words that would drive him away forever.

He reached over the table, covering her hand with his. "Would it help if I told you that over the past few days I've grown to admire you immensely? That I think you have courage and tenacity and a compassion that I am only starting to discover? That I've seen a caring side of you I never knew existed? That I'm starting to think that I may have judged you too harshly sometimes and that I'm sorry for that."

His eyes glowed with sincerity and a warmth she'd never seen before. Underneath his hand, hers felt safe, protected.

Oh, God.

"That I'm starting to like you very much indeed. And that I'd like to get to know you better. Much, much better."

Inside she'd turned to mush. His words pooled in the empty hole below her breastbone and created a warm glow. A hesitant joy started to blossom. She turned her hand upward and threaded her fingers through his.

"Yes," she said slowly. "I rather think it would." And she was half relieved, half frustrated when the waitress arrived at that moment with their main course.

They spent the balance of the meal exploring common interests, neither alluding to the bombshell Damon had dropped. Yet the knowledge of his declaration lay behind every glance, every exchange, and the air between them simmered.

He made her feel like a starry-eyed teenager on her first date. Ridiculous. She had to stop this. If Damon realised how bad she had it…

Rebecca laid her fork down with a clatter, glancing around to avoid meeting Damon's eyes until she'd managed to mask the elated anticipation in hers.

The windows were covered with heavy navy drapes printed with pale flowers that should have looked awful but instead echoed the gardens outside. In the corner stood a grand piano, and along the walls hung exquisite paintings of country scenes. The high ceiling gave a light, airy feel to the place.

"You know," she said suddenly, "this place would be perfect for the wedding."

Damon looked around. A quick dismissive glance. Then she felt the heat as his gaze returned to her face. "You are probably right."

She tried to ignore the pull of his attraction, focused on the idea she'd had.

"No *probably* about it. It *is* perfect!" Rebecca felt the familiar rising excitement which signified that a plan was coming together. "It would mean a smaller guest list than what your mother has planned. But it could work. This room would easily hold four hundred, and the covered veranda could seat another two hundred at least. The gardens are magnificent—Demetra would be in rhapsodies."

She turned to Damon. The instant their eyes met, a shock of awareness arced between them. He gave a slow smile that made her heart turn over. "I can see why you were so good at this business. You have a knack for matching people to places."

"No." She brushed his praise aside, tried to still the thumping of her heart. "It's just listening and observation." But the way he was looking at her intensified, until heat crept into her cheeks.

"You must know all the places, so where would you choose to get married?"

"I didn't know this one," she pointed out. "I have you to thank for that."

His smile stretched, lighting his eyes with a warm, intimate glow. "I cheated. It's only been open for a couple of years. Before that it was a private estate. You couldn't have known about it. You were up in Northland when it opened. Now tell me about your dream wedding."

"My dream wedding?" She stared at him, bemused.

"You used to successfully plan everyone else's—" he grinned "—dream occasions. What would you do for yourself?"

She laughed. "I blew it. Aaron and I had a civil wedding. No big deal." Aaron had wanted to get married the instant she'd said yes. There hadn't even been time to think, much less plan an elaborate A-list wedding.

Something moved in his blue eyes. "Okay, then fantasize. Tell me what you wish you'd done."

"My fantasy wedding..." Rebecca paused a moment, looking away from the beautiful blue gaze to gather her thoughts. "Well, for starters, I wouldn't need all this." She gestured to the high sash windows, the rich country-house decor. "I'd want something simple, just a ceremony and some time afterward with the man I married—the man I loved." She threw him a quick glance. "Too often weddings are tense occasions, and the bride is stressed half to death. I'd want time with the man I love to reflect on the solemn importance of the vows we'd just taken. I'd want them to be very, very permanent."

She could see she'd surprised him with her outburst. He looked startled. She'd revealed more about herself than she'd ever intended. For a moment she thought he was about to argue with her. To lighten the mood, she gave a light laugh and a shrug. "A fantasy is all it is. I won't be getting married."

"Why not?" He was frowning now, his eyes a clear, cool blue.

"I've already been married."

The blue clouded over. "That's a good reason not to marry again?"

She didn't want to talk about her marriage. Not to Damon. She shrugged again. "So what other reason is there? Children, I suppose. I've already got T.J."

"That's not the only reason people marry. There are things like companionship, understanding, love—"

"Oh, don't tell me you believe in all that fairy-tale stuff, Damon?" Rebecca interrupted, her smile sharp as she struggled not to let irony creep through.

"That's why Savvas and Demetra are getting married." He sat back, stirring his coffee.

"Yes, but they aren't like us. We're realists. We've seen the grittier side of life. Marriage is a financial deal, exchanging wealth for fidelity, the promise of children, isn't it?" It hurt to play devil's advocate, but it was nothing more than what Damon believed.

"God, you are cynical." He glared at her. "But even if you believe that, there's still sex. That's another reason people like *you* and *me*—" he drawled the words "—marry."

"Sex?" That one word was all it took. Her heartbeat took off, thundering inside her rib cage, her breathing shallow.

"Yes, hot sweaty sex. Body rubbing against body—"

"Oh, that kind of sex," she interrupted with a dismissive flutter of her hand, determined to put a stop to this before she started to pant, before he saw what he was doing to her. "But, Damon, I don't need to marry, I simply need to take a lover for that kind of sex."

Damon went rigid, his face a tight mask.

"And there have been many lovers?"

If he only knew!

She fluttered her eyelashes. "I *never* kiss and tell."

"No, of course you don't!" Disbelief underscored his derogatory words. "But you do kiss?"

"Oh, yes," she said breathlessly. "I can kiss."

The next thing she knew, he was out of his chair, beside her, leaning over. And then his mouth slanted across hers.

And she went up in flames.

There was no tenderness. It was a kiss that burned with hunger, desperation and need. He tasted of coffee, of cream, of everything she'd ever desired.

When he finally pulled away, he said slowly, "Oh, yes, you can kiss, all right."

There were betraying flags of heat across his cheekbones, his breath came in rapid bursts and his eyes glittered.

"Perhaps it *is* time you took a lover," he said darkly.

"Perhaps," she replied, bravely holding his gaze. "I'll need to start looking around."

"Oh no!" He was shaking his head, his teeth bared in a feral grin. "No, *koukla*, you will look no farther than me. I am going to be your lover."

Six

Hours later Rebecca still couldn't believe that she hadn't told Damon to go to blazes. Instead she'd retreated into a dazed silence, illicit excitement fluttering deep inside her belly. On the way home, Rebecca sank back into the rich butter-coloured leather seat and closed her eyes. She felt the touch of Damon's glance from time to time, but he didn't speak. An oppressive, sweltering awareness filled the Mercedes.

The moment the car swept into the drive of the Asteriades mansion, Rebecca sat up, muttered her thanks and, before they'd come to a standstill, bolted from the car. Hurrying to her room, she spent the next couple of hours—until Demetra and T.J. came home—making lists of what would be needed for the wedding, calls that needed to be made about brides-maids' dresses, flowers, catering. Anything to keep busy and stop herself thinking about Damon's outrageous proposition. Anything to keep her as far away from him as possible.

I am going to be your lover.

The arrogant statement still rang in her ears that evening as she helped T.J. into the bath. Contrarily, she was almost disappointed that Damon hadn't followed up, hadn't battered down the door to find out where she'd hidden herself all afternoon.

He was messing with her head. Why hadn't he sought her out?

Why had he made such a passionate proclamation in the first place?

He hated her.

But he'd said he'd actually come to like her. Rebecca closed her eyes to block out the confusion that whirled round and round inside her head. Without end. When she opened them again, T.J. was staring at her, holding out a soapy sponge. She took it and started to wash him.

"Mummy," T.J.'s piping voice cut into her dilemma. "Demetra's going to get big, fat fish with shiny—" he hesitated "—skin."

"Scales," Rebecca corrected automatically. T.J. had returned from his day with Demetra happy, tired and covered in mud, showing no sign that he'd missed her at all. Rebecca had heard all about the ducks in the park pond and about the fishpond he'd helped the workmen dig out at Demetra's soon-to-be home.

Her mind slid back into the rut it couldn't get out of. How could Damon change from hate to something as insipid as *like?* And how dare she be so grateful that he actually liked her, that he wanted to get to know her better. How could she be tempted to settle for that?

Damon said he wanted to be her lover. *Why?*

Yet, deep in the throbbing darkness of her womb, she knew. Chemistry. This thing between them that would never rest until it was sated. Liking her, getting to know her, was nothing more than a line.

A line to get her into his bed. Somehow he'd fathomed what she wanted more than anything in the world—his respect, his admiration…to be *liked* by him.

Pathetic.

A splash of water brought her back to reality. T.J. giggled.

She gave a mock growl and pulled his wet, wriggling body toward her. With one hand she reached for a towel and swaddled T.J., patting him dry.

What on earth was she going to do?

"And Demetra's got a net to the pond so the birds can't eat the fish."

She dragged her attention back to T.J. "No, if a heron took them, that would not be good." She started to towel T.J.'s hair.

"We fed ducks at the park. Very greedy ducks," he said reprovingly. "Demetra said next time we'll take two breads."

Just a few days and already T.J. was at home here in the bosom of Damon's family. It would be a wrench when the time came to go back home. He would feel bereft. Rebecca pressed a hasty kiss to the top of his head as misgivings quaked through her.

"Mummy, can we make a fishpond? Get some fish? And ducks? Please?"

"We'll see." Rebecca tried to smile. Perhaps a pond would help him adjust to the separation. T.J. was at that age where creatures and water fascinated him. He kept her on her toes during excursions, feeding ducks in the park ponds and peering into rock pools at the sea's edge. In a couple of years she'd have to buy him a fishing rod.

That was when he was going to miss having a father. What did she know about fishing, about hooks and sinkers and bait, after all? Rebecca sighed and hung up the towel. When she turned around, she saw T.J. had put on his pyjama bottoms back to front. She moved to help him.

"No, me do it," he said with a three-year-old's fierce determination.

She shook her head. Her baby was growing up—too fast— with no father figure to give him guidance. But he had her. He didn't need anyone else. And, as she had told Damon earlier, she had no reason for marrying. Ever. Especially not for sex.

And she was *not* going to be Damon's lover.

* * *

The weekend passed in a rush. On Saturday, Rebecca ushered T.J. into the dining room to find Damon had discarded his corporate attire and was wearing a pair of faded Levi's, a Ralph Lauren T-shirt in plain white…and a devastating smile aimed right at her.

Her stomach started doing somersaults.

"On Monday, I fly to L.A. on business, so I thought we might go for a picnic today."

Her heart sank. "But I wanted to spend time with T.J. I've barely seen—"

"Of course T.J. will come, too." Damon gestured to a wicker hamper she hadn't noticed. "Jane has already filled that with treats."

"Picnic, picnic," T.J. chanted, jumping up and down.

"He'll love that," Rebecca said, wondering why Damon was doing this.

They spent the day at Goat Island, a marine reserve an hour's drive out of Auckland. The sun was hot enough to prickle, and the sea frothed onto the curve of beach below the pohutukawa trees.

"It's hard to believe the city is so near," Rebecca commented as she and Damon stood in the shallows, the sea sand squishing through her toes and T.J. squealing with delight when blue mau-mau flashed between his ankles.

"When he is older, he can snorkel to the island." Damon pointed at the rocky outcrop that gave the reserve its name and sheltered the bay from the open sea.

Rebecca laughed. "He'll love that. He's a real water baby."

At noon they ate the delicious fare Jane had prepared, and afterward Rebecca lazed on a towel, her head propped against a beach bag, watching Damon and T.J. build sand castles. T.J. bubbled with joy and Damon, well, Damon took her breath away. From behind the protective cover of her sunshades she eyed the hard curves of his chest muscles, the flat abs and the muscled thighs kneeling in the sand. Her breathing picked up. She couldn't deny the effect he had on her.

Finally she admitted the truth to herself: she wanted him. She glanced away and focused on the waves licking the beach and struggled to remind herself that Damon was downright *dangerous*. She'd drowned in his attraction before. Why should it be any different this time?

Yet later, when he invited her out to dinner, she called herself all kinds of fool and accepted with a flush of pleasure. That night, after T.J. had been put to bed, they paid a short visit to Soula, leaving Demetra and Savvas to babysit. Soula took one look at the layered gypsy-style skirt and off-the-shoulder top that Rebecca wore and her gaze sharpened.

"You two going out?" she asked coyly.

"We have reservations at Shipwrecks. I promised Rebecca seafood tonight—"

"We took T.J. to Goat Island for the day," Rebecca said hastily, before Soula got the wrong idea. "I bewailed the fact that we could not fish in the reserve. So Damon insisted on taking me out for dinner."

"I see," Soula smiled sphinxlike, leaving Rebecca to wonder what she did indeed see.

Dinner passed in a haze. Damon was wonderful company. His eyes gleamed with appreciation when she spoke and he laughed often, his lips curving into that smile that made her knees go weak.

Rebecca had to remind herself that she had no intention of being charmed, of allowing Damon Asteriades to become her lover. Yet she didn't want the evening to end. But she knew it would and she rather suspected she knew how he intended it to end. So she was more than a little disconcerted when he said good-night to her outside her bedroom door without even brushing his lips across her cheek.

On Sunday morning he was waiting, a trip to the zoo planned this time. T.J. was in his element. He ran around, his eyes wide as he gazed at lions, elephants, rhinos, while Rebecca spent the day trying to keep her eyes off Damon. He appeared unaware of her growing tension, laughing with T.J. at the antics of the spider monkeys and the otters, oblivious of her acute sensitivity to the lightest brush of his hand.

That evening, after T.J. fell into bed, sun-flushed and tired, Rebecca couldn't help wondering where it was all going to end…and what on earth had happened to Damon's declaration that he wanted her.

After a hectic day escorting Demetra to half a dozen dress designers, Rebecca was surprised to find Damon at the dinner table on Monday night. Demetra was regaling Savvas and Damon with stories about how terrible the day had been, how she'd been tangled in yards of fabric and had pins stuck into her. Rebecca started to laugh.

"It's all your fault," Demetra accused, her eyes sparkling. "Admit it—you enjoyed yourself." Rebecca sat down between Savvas and Damon. T.J. was already in bed, fast asleep.

"Much more than I thought I would," Demetra conceded. "You knew what I would like."

"That's my job." Rebecca grinned at Demetra. Then to Damon, she said, "I thought you were flying out on a business trip today." She glanced down at the slice of melon on her plate. The last thing she wanted was Damon cottoning on to the fact that his every movement obsessed her.

"He was supposed to go to the States," Savvas responded. "But he's delayed it. He's got everyone in a flap about it because he needs to meet one of our American stakeholders."

"Next week." Damon's voice was short. "I told you I'll go next week."

"I can't understand what's so important that you have to be in Auckland this week."

"Don't worry yourself about it," Damon said in a peculiar tone.

Rebecca shot him a casual glance and froze. He was staring at her, his eyes burning. Her breath caught. Her pulse started to hammer. And she knew.

She was the reason he'd postponed his trip. Disjointed thoughts whirred round in her brain. So why hadn't he made a move on her? Why the outings with T.J. on the weekend and the dinner out if all he wanted was hot, sweaty sex?

She wished she could see inside his head, fathom what he was thinking.

But his intentions became no clearer with each day that followed. Each evening Damon would come home, play a little with her and T.J. and Demetra—sometimes Savvas would be there, too—and afterward he'd take her out. Once it was to see a movie she'd idly mentioned wanting to see, a couple of times he took her to dinner and on Thursday night he took her to a jazz concert. He was attentive, amusing and charming—a far cry from the hostile, critical man of the past. Rebecca was discovering a side of him that she'd never known existed. A side of him that made her crave more time in his company.

This was what she'd wanted—Damon to like her. For herself.

So that she could tell him the truth, so that he would believe she'd done what she had for the best reasons in the world, a little mischievous voice whispered. Because she'd wanted to spare him. But the man staring at her oozed confidence and power and far too much sex appeal for his own good. Her heart jolted. The blue eyes seared her, making her burn up inside and convincing her to push aside the little voice. Just a few days longer, she told herself, then she'd tell him. A few precious days to treasure this connection between them.

Because she knew it wouldn't last.

By Friday night Rebecca was ready to crack. It had been a busy week and she'd gotten lots done on the wedding. But it wasn't the wedding that had her in a tizz, it was Damon. Aside from the occasional hand under her elbow, he hadn't touched her, hadn't kissed her, and it was driving her mad.

She was confused. Out of her depth.

And she suspected he knew it.

They were meeting at seven on the deck for a drink. She'd forgotten to ask what they were doing tonight, forgotten to check if Demetra and Savvas could babysit T.J. No doubt Damon had it all under control. Like everything else in his life—including her.

Rebecca wasn't sure if she could endure another night out with the perfect escort…leaving her uncertain and yearning for more afterward.

It was seven o'clock on the dot when Rebecca stepped out through the ranch sliders onto the spacious raised deck overlooking the long sunken pool that reflected the crimson rays of the sinking sun.

Something tightened in Damon's chest as she paused, stilling for an instant before she stepped forward. A pair of black pants in a soft fabric swirled around her legs, and she wore high strappy sandals that made her look tall and lithe and incredibly sexy. His gazed moved up to the peacock-blue shirt that hugged her lush breasts, lingering briefly at the unbuttoned vee neckline where a blue opal set in gold dangled against her creamy skin. His brows contracted at the sight of the expensive pendant. *Soon she would be his.* She would wear jewellery he bought for her, not baubles from other men.

He leashed the primal wave of possessiveness that flooded him and jerked his eyes back to her face. "A punctual woman," he drawled. "A pearl beyond price."

She looked unsettled. Then she smiled her slow, sexy smile and heat kicked through him. He forgot about the opal, about the man who'd bought it for her.

"Old habits die hard," she said, sitting down on the chair he'd drawn up for her and taking the glass of white wine he held out with a smile of thanks.

"Yes, I remember that about you. You always had a reputation for being professional in your business dealings." He frowned. Her private reputation had been very different indeed.

A shadow fell across her face.

"What are you thinking?" He couldn't rid himself of this compulsion to delve into her thoughts, crawl under her skin to find out what made her tick.

"Nothing," she said. She touched the opal at her neck.

"Tell me."

She drew a breath. "It was Aaron who drilled the importance of punctuality into me. Your comment made me remember how much he taught me."

Damon forced himself not to glance at the pendant. He didn't want to think about her dead husband any more than he wanted to think about his dead wife. He didn't want the past or the future intruding. All he wanted was tonight—and the intriguing woman sitting beside him.

His woman. From tonight.

Until he tired of her. As he knew he would. It couldn't be otherwise.

He moved his chair closer and changed the subject. "What do you think of the wine?"

Rebecca lifted the glass to her lips. "Mmm. Buttery. Like a good Chardonnay should be." She held the glass up against the last rays of the evening light. The liquid turned to pure gold. "Good colour, too." Another sip. "Chilled. There's a hint of something else there...something slightly sweet."

"Melon? Pineapple?" Damon found he enjoyed teasing her.

She slanted him a wry look. "Honey, I think."

"Honey?"

Honey reminded him of that too-brief kiss they'd shared

at lunch the other day. She had tasted of honey. Sweet. Addictive. He could feel his eyes darkening, could feel the heavy languor in his limbs as he remembered the desire that had forked through him.

Rebecca had gone utterly still, caught in the same intense thrall that ensnared him. She gave a shiver and rubbed her arms.

"Cold?" he asked softly. But he knew it wasn't cold that had caused the rows of goose bumps that disappeared under the sleeves of her shirt. It was excitement. The same raw excitement that writhed within him.

She shook her head.

"Rebecca—"

"Where's Demetra?" she interrupted. "Where's Savvas?"

He sat back, forced himself to relax, to take it slowly. One step at a time. "Demetra said she wanted to see glowworms, so Savvas whipped her away to Waitomo. They plan to go blackwater rafting as well. They won't be back until Sunday afternoon at the earliest." He grinned wickedly. "There's no need to wait up for them."

"What about Jane? I'd hate to think she's waiting for us to eat." Rebecca sounded rattled. She took another quick sip of wine, leaned forward to set her glass down on the patio table.

He moved closer, enjoying her loss of composure. He wanted to see her abandon her cool, her poise. "Jane left about half an hour ago for the weekend. She prepared a cold spread. We'll eat when you're ready. The night is still young."

"And Johnny?"

"Johnny's gone to tea at his daughter's—he is a grandfather twice over now. He'll be back tomorrow."

He waited.

She didn't disappoint him. Her eyes widened, darkening as the import of his words struck her. "That means…" Her voice became husky, trailed off.

"That we are alone."

She stared wordlessly at him, her eyes huge, dark and velvety.

He placed a hand over hers. Her fingers were icy. "Except for T.J.—"

"He's...he's sleeping," she stuttered.

"Then, yes, we are alone."

She shuddered convulsively.

He let his fingers stroke over the back of her hand, softly, over her pale bare wrists, up her arm. The sleek, silky material of her sleeve clung to his fingers. His hand rested against the soft skin of her throat and then he placed his index finger under her chin. Her head tilted up.

Her lovely eyes were wary, but beneath the uncertainty there was a flare of fire.

"You know what I plan to do, don't you?"

"Yes." A whisper.

But it was enough for Damon. He bent forward until only an infinitesimal space separated them. "I'm going to kiss you," he murmured.

He brushed her lips.

Lightly.

It was a kiss meant to tease. Except it backfired on him. Instead of teasing her, it made him want more. Much, much more.

When Rebecca sighed, her lips parting, Damon could wait no longer. With a hungry groan he took her mouth, possessing it. He forgot to take it slowly, he forgot to be patient, he forgot about courting her. His tongue swept in to taste her sweetness. Like honey, wild and golden. And then he forgot everything as the hot fury of passion rushed over him.

He pulled her toward him, onto his lap.

Her body was soft, feminine against the hard planes of his, he was aware that she was moaning, and the sound spurred him on. To taste deeper. To kiss wilder.

After a while—he didn't know how long—he lifted his

head. His hands were shaking. He struggled with the button at her neckline. It gave. He slid his hand in and cupped her breast. Heard her breath catch.

The tip was hard against his fingers. He caught it between his fingertips, caressed it softly, circling the sensitive bud.

She gasped again. He covered her mouth. Devoured her. This time her tongue was wild against his, rubbing, playing, arousing.

He touched her, working the nipple, feeling the frantic bursts of shivers that ripped through her. He was hard under his jeans. Every time she wriggled her bottom in his lap he moaned, growing hotter and hotter.

His breathing was ragged when he forced himself to pull back.

Unbelievable. The desire that surged made him feel like a boy. Hasty. Impulsive. Out of control.

"Come." He rose to his feet, letting her slide down the length of his chest, aware of every soft curve of her pliant body. Taking her hand, he led her toward the open ranch sliders, where voile curtains billowed.

"Where—?"

"It will be warmer inside, the sea breeze is rising."

"What—"

Her eyes were wild, blind with passion.

"Tonight…I'm going to become your lover."

She gaped at him.

He wanted her to know, to know who he was and what was going to happen between. "Your lover, Rebecca."

"Yes."

That was what he'd been waiting for. Her capitulation. Her total commitment. He wanted her willing, he wanted her wanton. Because he intended to make her lose every vestige of control, he wanted to see the woman under the facade. The woman none of her other lovers had seen.

He wanted her as far out of control as he was.

* * *

"Your skin is so soft." His touch was surprisingly tender as he parted the final buttons of her shirt. He drew an exploratory finger across her torso, under her breasts, and a line of fire followed.

Rebecca lay on his bed fully clothed, only her sandals kicked off...and the necklace that Damon had removed with impatient, shaking fingers. Her head spun from the kisses he'd pressed on her mouth, her cheeks, her neck. Yet nothing had prepared her for this...

His touch.

The fire.

She caught her lip between her teeth, fought the wild sensation that arced through her.

"Tell me what you like, what turns you on. I want to know everything about you." His hand slid under her bra, brushed across the nipple. She stopped breathing.

"You like that?" Something akin to triumph glittered in his eyes.

She suppressed the urge to nod and stared at him, hoping her eyes didn't reveal what he was doing to her or how much she'd craved his touch.

But her body gave her away.

"You love it!" He drew that teasing finger back over the dark tip, and the nipple tightened, bringing a prickle close to pain. Rebecca groaned.

Damon pushed her shirt aside, off her shoulders, slid his hand behind her and then her breasts were free. "Beautiful. Such fullness, such softness." He touched the curves with strong hands that were oddly gentle.

Against her will, her back arched, pushing her breasts into his hands. Damon stared as if transfixed, then his head dropped and his mouth closed over the peak.

The sensation that exploded within Rebecca was like nothing she'd ever felt before. It flashed through her belly, between her legs, heating her, setting her on fire.

A groan burst from her as his tongue flicked. Another flick. Another flash of fire.

A groan tore from her throat.

He lifted his head, and the expression on his face caused her mouth to dry. Desire stretched his face into a pagan mask. His eyes gleamed and the curve of his mouth was softened by passion. His whole attention focused on her.

Nothing but her.

This was the man she'd always craved.

She twisted her hips, and he seemed to know exactly what she wanted because he shifted so that his weight covered her, heavy and erotic.

The hardness of his erection filled the cradle between her legs as if it belonged, the other half of her. Heat ignited. She leaned forward, kissed his cheek hungrily, following the line of his jaw to nuzzle behind his ear, heard him moan and let her lips open against his neck. He tasted salty, male. She licked him, eager to taste more.

His big, strong body shuddered against her. He moved against her, the hardness beneath his jeans sliding against the soft mound covered by her satin black pants.

She felt the zip give, then his hand was moving in wide sweeps and her pants and panties were gone. A rasp of a second zipper and his jeans and shirt followed suit. Their bare legs tangled, his male and muscled against the softness of her thighs.

Her legs jerked apart. Instantly he edged into the space. The maddening friction notched higher, driving her wilder and wilder, up and up, heat and want and a ceaseless pressure spiralling within her.

Restlessly she spread her legs wider still.

"You're hot for me."

She didn't speak, didn't respond to his harsh statement,

simply rotated her hips against him and tried to get closer, closer, so that he could touch the heart of her.

"You want me, don't you?"

Something in the insistence of his tone brought her down a little. Opening her eyes, she found his face above hers, his blue eyes boring into hers.

"Say it, Rebecca! Tell me how much you want me."

"I want you…."

"I want more. Tell me more."

More? She shook herself. What did he want?

His face was taut, sweat glowing on his cheekbones. There was no hint of softness. No tenderness. No I—

Surely Damon couldn't be waiting for her to tell him she loved him. Or could he? Could she expose herself to him? Give him that kind of power over her?

Dare she risk it?

She tilted her pelvis, firming the taut connection between them. He gasped, closed his eyes, threw his head back.

"God, what you do to me!"

Exhilarated, she moved again.

"Why, dammit? Why you?" The cry was filled with ecstasy and agony. And revealed a vulnerability that she knew he'd never have shown any other time. A vulnerability she was certain he'd regret revealing later.

Suddenly Rebecca knew what he wanted. Snaking her arms around his neck, she pulled his head down to hers. "It's mutual. I want you, too, Damon, more than I've ever wanted anyone," she whispered.

"Anyone?"

"Anyone," she vowed.

"Much more?"

"Much, much more," she affirmed, her arms tightening fiercely.

He gave a hissing sigh and sank into her.

Rebecca cried out.

She told herself he cared for her. He wouldn't be doing this if he didn't. Not like this. He wouldn't be so determined that it should be…more…than ever before if it meant nothing to him.

This was something he'd never felt before. She had to believe that. Otherwise…

He started to move. She shuddered, opened herself wider, forcing the junction of her thighs close to him, trying to become one with him.

He lowered his torso, the contact sensitising her breasts until she almost cried out again. She bit down hard on her bottom lip, wildly conscious of the heat rising deep within in her.

The pressure where their bodies joined was growing…growing…the heat rising higher. She could bear it no more. She ground herself against him, heard him gasp, felt his shudders.

"I can't hold back," he panted.

"Come," she whispered. "Come with me. Stay with me. Always." He opened his eyes. She read confusion. She moved, slow and sinuous, and the confusion vanished. There was passion and heat in the blue depths…and something deep and unfathomable.

And then all rational thought vanished and the shivers seized her. She fell through layers of sensation, felt his body freeze, then release into pulsing convulsions as he came deep within her.

Afterward they dozed for a while. When Rebecca woke, the red digital numbers on Damon's bedside clock revealed that it was after midnight.

"T.J." She leaped from the pile of scattered bedclothes.

Damon caught her hand. "He's still sleeping, I checked. Stay."

The heat in his eyes, the hoarseness in his voice told her what he intended.

"I can't." She looked away. And she felt herself weakening, but guilt ate at her.

"Rebecca, I want you." His admission caused her to melt. She turned to him. No words were necessary. Before she'd lain down, he fell on her. This time their loving was wild, uncontrolled. There were no barriers between them. No past. No future. Only the present.

Yet she knew that soon a new day would dawn. Tomorrow…tomorrow they would talk. She could delay no longer, she had to tell him the truth.

When the first pale strands of daylight slid into the room Rebecca rose and pulled on her clothes. Damon slept, his breathing deep and rhythmic. Standing beside him, she resisted the urge to kiss the shadowed groove under his jaw and touch the smooth curve of his shoulder. Instead she picked her pendant off his bedstand and, leaving her feet bare, padded to the door, sandals in hand, and quietly shut the door behind her.

Once in her room, she crossed to the adjacent dressing room. The dawn cast a soft pink glow across the walls. T.J. had tossed the bedclothes off and lay on his stomach, his face turned to the door. She bent and brushed a kiss on his brow, whispered "I love you," then pulled the blankets up to cover him.

She didn't go to bed immediately but stood at the open window of her room staring at the rosy streaks lightening the darkness, the pendant clutched in her hand. Something in Damon's eyes had told her that he didn't care for the pendant. She would not wear it again. It was time to say goodbye to Aaron, to think about the future.

And Damon.

Last night had been the most tender, the most passionate, the most incredible experience of her life.

She'd gone wild in Damon's arms. She feared she'd revealed too much. How would he react when he next saw her? Oh, God. How was she going to tell him what she knew she had to? He was going to hate her. After last night, she didn't know how she could go back to that half-life where he despised her.

She turned from the window. Carefully she placed the pendant in the jewel box on her dressing table and closed the lid. The rasp of the hasp sounded so final. Rebecca placed a kiss of her fingertips and let them linger for a moment on the carved lid.

After a brief sojourn to the bathroom, Rebecca donned her nightgown, aware of her body aching in unaccustomed places. A pleasurable ache. Her thoughts shifted to Damon. She could barely believe what had taken place between them.

The passion. The frenzy.

Yet there had been gentleness, too. She slipped between the Egyptian cotton sheets and let herself remember. The first time his touch had been so careful, tender even. So far removed from how he'd treated her in the past. Whether that tenderness would still be there after they talked, she was too scared to even think about.

Tomorrow would come soon enough.

Seven

The sound of screaming woke Rebecca.

Shrill, childish screams followed by a chilling silence. The door to T.J.'s room stood wide-open and her bedroom door was ajar onto the corridor. She leaped up, the thick mists of sleep falling rapidly away.

"T.J.?"

There was no answer. Fear galvanised her into action. She hurtled into his room. Trains lay scattered across the carpet. Thomas…Henry…Gordon. A wild glance took in T.J.'s favourites. But no T.J.

Terror released a wave of adrenaline, her knees turning to liquid. Rebecca burst out into the corridor, uncaring that she still wore nightclothes.

"T.J.!" Rebecca was yelling now, her voice hoarse with shock. She rushed down the stairs. At the bottom she paused. The large double-height lobby led to the solid carved front door and beyond that lay the road. To the right lay Soula's rooms, and in the opposite direction another corridor led to the entertainment rooms and the kitchen.

She heard shouts. An adult this time. Coming from outside. It sounded like...Johnny. A swift glance at her watch showed her that it was a little before seven.

She started to run.

A large male form brushed past her. A blur of flesh wearing only a pair of boxers and moving at breakneck speed.

Damon.

Then he was gone, tearing into the lounge as if all the hounds of hell were after him.

Rebecca had a brief recollection of billowing curtains, of the open ranch sliders, and a sick, swirling sense of horror filled her.

"Please, no. Oh, God. *T.J.*" She burst out onto the deck in time to see Damon disappear under the water, heard the resounding splash. Her shell-shocked gaze swept the deck, the pool.

Where was T.J.?

Johnny was also in the water. Incongruous in his sodden black blazer and limp tie, his thinning hair plastered to his scalp, his eyes worried.

So where was T.J.?

Someone was screaming, an unending, unearthly howl of grief. Johnny held up a hand, beckoning urgently. Only then did Rebecca realise it was her—she was screaming. Wailing. The scream died abruptly. She scurried to the water's edge.

"Wait," Johnny shouted. "Don't jump in. Call the ambulance. Call Dr. Campbell—his number is on the handset. The boss will get the youngster out."

Shaking with reaction, she ran blindly back to the lobby, snatched up the cordless phone and dialled 111 with fumbling fingers. "Hurry, hurry," she prayed, and dry sobs of relief racked her when the operator came on the line.

Rebecca gave the details and the location in a blur. Her fingers shook as she punched out the next number. Dr. Campbell's receptionist promised to send him immediately.

Rebecca rushed out onto the deck again, dropping the handset at the sight of Damon emerging from the water, T.J. struggling in his arms.

T.J. Her baby was alive! Her vision blurred. She scrubbed at her eyes and her hands came away wet. She tore across to where Damon was laying T.J. down on the terra-cotta pavers. T.J. was retching and then the screaming started—the most welcome sound Rebecca had ever heard.

"I'm here, baby." Rebecca fell to her knees. A tear plopped onto T.J.'s pale skin, mingling with rivulets of water from the pool. "Thank God."

"T.J. Oh, T.J., I am so sorry."

The ambulance and Dr. Campbell had been and gone. T.J. lay on the couch, asleep, exhausted from the toll the shock and the crying jag had taken on his system. Rebecca hunched over her son, her back tense and shaking, her anguish palpable. From time to time she stroked T.J. with hands that trembled, as if to assure herself he was alive.

Rebecca who never cried.

Coming to a decision, Damon strode to her. Without giving her an opportunity to resist, he swept her into his arms. Crossing to the sofa opposite the one T.J. occupied, he lowered himself, fitting Rebecca into his lap.

"Dr. Campbell says he's fine."

"I know, but I can't seem to stop. When I think what might have happened...God!" Her whole body started to shake.

Holding her, he rocked her. "Don't think. It achieves nothing."

She drew a deep, heaving breath and buried her face in his chest, into the black T-shirt he'd hurriedly shrugged on after Dr. Campbell had checked T.J. out.

He braced himself for more tears. "Hush, you'll make yourself ill."

No tears came, but the tremors grew worse. "You don't understand. I nearly lost him."

He did understand. How to tell her? He hated the helplessness that swamped him. Nothing he could say, do, would take away her pain. In silent sympathy he tightened his arms around her and said inadequately, "He'll be fine."

She sniffed against his chest. "It's my fault."

"No, it's mine. I should have thought about that door." Damon stared bleakly over her head. Last night he'd plotted the seduction of the woman he held in his arms. He'd been so intent on her, on his pleasure, that he'd forgotten about the blasted sliders. After he'd promised Rebecca they would remain locked at all times, he'd let her down. Rebecca's son had paid for his carelessness.

Nearly with his life.

"It should never have happened," she choked.

"It won't happen again." He went cold as he relived those horrible moments.

"I mean—" she lifted her woebegone face "—it wouldn't have happened if I'd been a better mother."

The immaculate mask had been torn away. Still clad in her nightie, her hair tangled, her eyes red-rimmed from crying, she had never looked more vulnerable nor more beautiful.

He brushed his lips across her smooth brow. "Don't blame yourself. If anyone is at fault, it's me for assuming that it would be simple to keep the sliders closed—after all, they latch automatically. I know better now. And I know that you couldn't possibly be a better mother."

She hiccupped. "I'm a terrible mother. I'm a total failure as a mother, I always knew I would be. I've failed—"

"Rebecca." He gave her a shake. "Listen to me! No one can doubt your commitment to T.J. You're patient, loving. What more could a child want?"

But instead of calming her, his praise simply made her sob, her dark eyes spilling tears that wrenched his heart.

"I don't deserve T.J."

"You know, if you'd asked me four years ago what kind of

mother I thought you'd be, I would have said appalling. Selfish. But I've watched you with T.J. You've astounded me. You've impressed me. I admire your patience. Even when he's being downright difficult, you always do the right thing."

"I'm not a natural mother."

"You could have fooled me." With a gentle hand, he stroked her hair.

But the gesture did little to calm her. Instead she only cried harder. "You don't understand!"

"Try me."

"No. I can't." She sat up in his lap, shaking her head wildly so that her long hair whipped around her tear-drenched face. "There are things…things I haven't told you. Things you should've known before we…before we slept together."

"Shush. Don't worry about that now."

"I must." Her teeth were clattering. "Ignoring it won't make it go away. I'm so scared—"

He yanked her back against his chest, so close that he could feel her hot breath against his chest. He scanned her uptilted features, concerned about the misery, the guilt he read there. "Stop this. You'll make yourself ill!"

Remorse flashed across her face, making her look even more wretched. "And then what good will I be to T.J.?"

"That can't be self-pity I hear, is it? Come on, buckle up."

She gave him a watery smile. "You mean buck up."

He shrugged. "Whatever."

Rebecca made a valiant effort to pull herself together. Pulling away, she perched on the edge of his lap and examined him. "*Whatever?* You're always so formal I sometimes forget that you only arrived here in New Zealand when you were— what—eight? Nine?"

"Ten," he corrected, looking surprised at the change of subject. "My father saw New Zealand as a land of opportunity. When I arrived, neither Savvas nor I could speak any English. Where were you when you were ten, Rebecca?"

"With the Austins. They were one of the better foster families I stayed with." But that was when she'd been parted from James. The Austins had two daughters and didn't want to foster boys. They hadn't minded taking two girls into care. The other girl had been Fliss. Poor shell-shocked Fliss who had recently lost her parents in a freak boating accident. Separated from James for the first time in her life, Rebecca had shared Fliss's bewildered sense of loss. It had been natural that the two of them had clung to each other.

"How many foster homes did you stay in?"

"Altogether? Four," she said bleakly.

He pulled her back into his arms. "You know, T.J. is very fortunate to have you for a mother."

"No, I'm the lucky one. It's easy to love him." She glanced up at him as she spoke and her eyes were luminous with profound emotion, and for an instant Damon felt a pang of envy at her bond of love with the child. He pushed it aside.

His voice rough with emotion, he said, "You're a wonderful mother. I've watched you. Never think you're a failure as a mother."

Wonder lit her eyes. "Thank you, Damon. That means a lot to me. More than you could ever know, because my mother abandoned James and me, and we never knew who fathered us."

"You're not your mother. You've done wonders. He's a son to be proud of." He brushed a kiss across the top of her head. It didn't matter who her parents were. But it explained her fierce determination to be independent. Every word he'd spoken was true. She *had* surprised him. At first he'd assumed the mothering thing was all an elaborate act. An empty charade. But slowly he'd seen the depth of her love for T.J., and for some reason the bond between them highlighted the emptiness of his own life. He'd enjoyed the trip to Goat Island, the visit to the zoo. Much to his astonishment, Damon found *he* wanted to be included in the intimate moments of warmth they shared, to be part of the unbreakable bond.

Rebecca stayed close to T.J. all day.

Damon had carried him upstairs to his room and he'd slept until well after midday. When T.J. finally awoke, he'd been tearful and told Rebecca emphatically that he never, ever wanted to swim ever again.

Hugging his shivering body, Rebecca hoped that it would be a temporary aversion and made a mental note to arrange him a course of swimming lessons after a little time had elapsed. Then they'd settled down to play with the brightly painted trains on the wooden tracks.

Several hours later a light rap at the door caused them both to raise their heads. The door swung open. Damon stood there looking oddly hesitant. "Dr. Campbell just rang. The hospital is discharging my mother tomorrow morning."

"You must be thrilled." Rebecca gave up trying to manoeuvre Gordon through the signal crossing and sat back on her heels. "Is she strong enough?"

He shrugged. "Dr. Campbell thinks she's fine. He also wanted to check on T.J. I told him that T.J. had eaten, that you were with him. You're welcome to phone him later if you're worried about anything." Damon's assessing glance flickered over T.J. "May I come in?"

"Want to play trains?" T.J. invited, blissfully unaware of the growing tension.

"May I?"

T.J. nodded enthusiastically. "The green train is Henry. The black engine is Diesel. He's being naughty today."

Damon squatted on the floor. "Naughty? Why? What did he do?"

Rebecca waited, heart pounding under her throat.

T.J. didn't look up. "He fell in the duck pond."

Damon went white. "T.J.—"

"He did it on purpose because he wanted to swim."

Rebecca drew a cautious breath. "Maybe Diesel needs a couple of swimming lessons?"

"No." T.J. was adamant. "Diesel never wants to swim again."

Damon shot Rebecca a helpless glance over T.J.'s head.

"Diesel loves to swim, just like you do. Lessons will help him swim better," Rebecca said calmly.

"What if he's scared?"

Damon pushed the Chinese Dragon along the track. "It's fine to be scared, T.J. Everyone gets scared sometimes."

"Not you—you're a man. A big growed-up man. You don't get scared," T.J. replied with childish logic.

Rebecca fought the smile that threatened to break out across her face at the observation. Damon *was* a man, every muscled inch of him.

"Even me," Damon said emphatically. "I get scared, too. I've been very scared because my mother has been ill. And I was scared this morning, too."

"I scared, too," T.J. said. Wide round eyes looked up at the man crouched beside him.

"Nothing wrong with that, son."

Rebecca sagged. Watching Damon with T.J., she couldn't believe how well he'd handled that. She'd been treading on eggshells all day, terrified of bringing up the subject, yet knowing that it would be healthier for T.J. to discuss it rather than let it fester.

Gratitude filled her—and something more. Something that made her throat thicken, a warm sweet feeling with a bitter edge that made tears threaten.

Dear God, how she loved this man.

The emotion she felt now was stronger than almost four years ago. More compelling than the fierce attraction that had drawn her to Damon all those years ago. Then she'd fallen madly in lust with him.

And thought it love until it had turned to pain.

Pain that had shattered her.

It wasn't the same as what she felt now. Then she'd only recognised Damon's sensual magnetism, glimpsed the passion beneath the tight control.

She'd accused him of judging her without getting to know her. Well, she hadn't known him, either. Not beyond the fierce pull he held over her body. She'd pursued him with headstrong recklessness—and paid the price.

The price had been his contempt.

Over the recent weeks she'd gotten to know him. Really know him. Not just the sexy, charismatic Greek male she'd been wildly infatuated with years before. But the real man under the corporate billionaire mask. Had grown to understand his fierce loyalty, the protective love with which he guarded his loved ones. This morning Damon had done everything in his power to rescue T.J.

T.J. was under his roof, so he felt responsible for what had happened. Even though they'd both been there. Not once had he blamed her for leaving the sliders open. Without a word he'd assumed the full mantle of guilt.

And now, watching him playing trains with T.J., their dark heads close together, she recognised the essence of his strength and his capacity to show care and tenderness to a child—a child of a woman for whom he'd had little respect in the past. A woman who was now his lover.

The woman who loved him with an intensity of feeling that scorched her. And this time it was more than lust. This love had the depth of an adult, confident woman. This was the love of a mother who trusted a strong, dominant male not to harm her child, to protect them both to the limits of his strength, with his life if necessary.

Damon was the man for her. So strong, so passionate, so gentle. A man that a woman would be proud to have beside her for all the years of her life. There would be no other man for her.

There never had been.

* * *

That night, once T.J. was sleeping, Đamon insisted that Rebecca come downstairs for a break after spending the whole day closeted upstairs.

Damon had given Johnny time off to allow Rebecca some privacy and space to recover from the morning's trauma. Once Johnny vanished to his quarters, they were alone. Savvas and Demetra would only be back tomorrow afternoon, and Damon had decided against calling them. They would find out soon enough about T.J.'s brush with tragedy.

Now, as she sat curled up on the sofa opposite him, Damon saw that her eyes were bruised with tiredness. While he was tempted to sit down beside her and pull her into his arms he resisted the temptation lest she think he was prompted by lust. Sex was the last thing Rebecca needed right now.

"Are you okay?"

She glanced up at him and nodded. There were grooves of tension beside her mouth and her face was full of hollows. The long, tempestuous day had been hard on her.

He ached to kiss the strain away. All his preconceptions were under attack. The woman he'd once considered vain and selfish was a devoted mother. She was kind to his mother. Yet thinking back to the past, he could remember instances where she'd been fiercely protective of Felicity. To the point where she'd confronted him, pleaded with him not to marry Felicity. He'd been enraged when she'd accused him of coercing Felicity into a marriage that she'd regret. He'd dismissed Rebecca's pleas as machinations, an attempt to get what she wanted: *him.* But now he was no longer sure that it had been all about him. Perhaps—

"Damon…" Rebecca interrupted his thoughts.

"Yes?"

"It doesn't matter." She looked away, a vivid flush staining her pale skin.

"What is it?"

"Will you hold me?" The words came out in a rush and the eyes that met his were shadowed by uncertainty.

"Of course!" He moved to sit beside her. Looping an arm around her shoulders, he pulled her close. She nestled her head against his chest with a soft sigh. She smelled of talcum powder and something sweet. He had a strong urge to tilt her face up to his and kiss her breathless. He killed the impulse and pressed a tame, gentle kiss against her hair instead.

His thoughts drifted back to the past. Why had Rebecca been so set against his marriage? Why had Felicity left? Had Rebecca known something that he hadn't? Rebecca had been right about one thing: Felicity had not been happy married to him. She'd tried to hide it with demure smiles. And failed miserably.

It had frustrated him. He'd showered his bride with gifts. She'd accepted them, but he'd sensed a...sadness in her. He'd given her his attention, escorted her to plays, the finest restaurants, everything that a woman who had grown up poor should have revelled in. Everything except his love.

Had her unhappiness been his fault? At the time he hadn't considered that. Too soon she'd been gone. And he'd been furious, humiliated that his bride of six weeks had deserted him. He'd blamed Rebecca. Hated her for publicly emasculating him.

He'd wanted to go after her. But his mother had told him he needed time to get some perspective. Soula had argued that Felicity's desertion couldn't possibly be Rebecca's doing. He hadn't had the heart to disagree, but his resentment of Rebecca had grown like a cancer within him—and then Felicity had died.

Felicity's casket. Strewn with waxen white flowers.

He hadn't spoken to anyone except his family at the funeral. He hadn't stayed after the burial in case he'd taken Rebecca apart with his bare hands where she stood motionless beside the raw ochre earth at the cemetery, as immaculate as ever, only her red-rimmed eyes revealing that Felicity had meant anything to her at all.

By the next day he'd calmed down and she'd been gone. Vanished. Before he could mete out the accounting. It would've been easy enough to have his security agency locate her, to drag her back. Instead he'd let her go. Because he'd known that his fury was beyond tempering, that his reaction would've cost him more than he dared risk—the loss of his self-control.

He shook his head furiously to clear it of the stranglehold of the past. It was dead, dead, dead. Just like Felicity. It was time to move on. And Rebecca was very much alive, her body soft and warm in the curve of his arms. Damon rested his unshaven cheek against her head and rubbed it back and forth.

"Damon?"

"Mmm?" he murmured.

"Will you make love to me?"

"Now?" His body kicked into action despite his disbelief.

"If you don't mind."

"Mind? Of course I don't mind." He wished he could see her face. Already his body was reacting, hardening. "Are you sure that's what you want?"

"I've had the worst day of my life. I want to…to do something that will help me forget. To put some distance between this morning and tomorrow. Is it terrible to seek oblivion in your body?"

"No…" he croaked, then swallowed and found his voice. "No, it's not terrible at all." Pulling her into his lap, he said, "Tell me what I can do to make the pain go away."

"Just love me."

Rebecca sounded so despairing that he groaned and dipped his head to kiss her. Tonight he'd help her forget, Damon vowed. He'd wipe the shadows from her eyes and let passion replace her pain.

T.J.'s hold tightened on Rebecca's hand as they entered the house shortly before noon on Sunday. Rebecca couldn't help wondering if something of her own nervous excitement at the thought of seeing Damon again had communicated itself to T.J.

Last night's lovemaking had been slow, gentle and immensely satisfying. She'd fallen asleep wrapped in Damon's arms. By the time T.J.'s stirring had woken her this morning, Damon had already gone from her bed, the sound of splashing telling her he was swimming his daily laps. It didn't take Rebecca long to pull on a pair of crisp white shorts and a red tank top. With trainers on her feet and her hair loose about her shoulders, she and T.J. had gone down to breakfast. Damon had come into the dining room, his hair still towel-damp. His light kiss had been full of warm affection that had caused her stomach to flip-flop. After breakfast, her spirits high, she and T.J. had walked down to a nearby park while Damon went to the hospital to fetch Soula.

"It's okay," Rebecca reassured T.J. now as they crossed the airy lobby. "We're not going onto the deck or anywhere near the pool." T.J.'s steps slowed at the mention of the pool. Hurriedly Rebecca distracted him, "Remember I told you about Damon's mother?"

T.J. nodded.

"Well, you can come and meet her now. I can hear her voice. She's home from hospital." Rebecca hesitated. *Kyria Asteriades* was too much of a mouthful for a child of Damon's age. "You can call her *Kyria* Soula. Or maybe just *Kyria*."

T.J. baulked for an instant then followed Rebecca into the lounge. Damon was seated at a right angle to his mother, conversing in rapid Greek. His jagged profile stood out, harsh and barbaric amidst the immaculate, subdued decor of the room.

A pirate in civilised surroundings.

Her lover.

Flushing, Rebecca led T.J. further into the formal room. Damon broke off and rose to his feet. The smile he sent her was exquisitely warm. T.J. crept forward from where he'd huddled behind her legs.

"Come," Damon said and switched the warm, comforting smile to T.J.

Despite the horror of the previous day, a glow of something approaching happiness surrounded Rebecca. Giving T.J.'s hand a gentle squeeze, she walked forward.

"Soula, no, don't stand up." Rebecca let go of T.J.'s hand and waved Damon's mother back to the couch. She glanced at the teapot and the empty cups beside the plate of shortbread on the coffee table. "Can I pour you another cup of tea? How are you feeling?"

"No more tea for me. I'm much better for being home, *pethi*. I'm tired of lying, sitting. I need to stretch my legs." Damon's mother rose and embraced Rebecca.

Rebecca inhaled the elegant floral perfume Soula wore. Feminine, classy, slightly old-world. After a moment Soula stepped back to peer past Rebecca. "Where is your boy?"

With a sense of inevitability, Rebecca watched Soula's jaw drop.

"*The mou*. Those eyes! My God. He's the spitting image of—" Her shocked gaze met Rebecca's.

Rebecca stared back. Hoping, praying, that Soula would not let the cat out the bag, that she'd keep what she'd seen to herself.

Soula cast Damon a fleeting glance and flashed a calculating look at Rebecca. Then she swung around to her son, her arms outstretched. "*Ye mou*, you should have told me."

Damon looked thoroughly at sea. "Told you what, Mama?"

"That you and Rebecca have a child!"

Rebecca's own shock was nothing compared to that mirrored on Damon's face.

"*A child?* What are you talking about, Mama?"

Soula clasped a hand over her mouth. "You do not know?"

"Know? Know what?" But his gaze was already flickering between T.J., Rebecca and Soula. Rebecca could see him putting it all together in that lightning-swift brain.

"No." Rebecca stepped forward. "Soula, you have it—"

"I'm so happy!" Soula kissed Damon on the cheek and draped an arm around him. "This is what I have longed for. My grandchild. Rebecca, come." She motioned with her arm and hugged her close, including her in the circle. "You have made an old woman so happy. I have prayed for years you two would realise the terrible tension between you is not hatred."

Rebecca didn't dare look at Damon.

"The child is baptised?" Soula asked.

Rebecca nodded, trying to ignore the tension that vibrated in Damon's body beside her.

"But not in the Greek Orthodox faith," Soula stated. "We need to attend to that. You two will need to get married. I cannot have Iphegenia and the rest of my family gossiping."

Soula's words shocked Rebecca to the core. *Marriage? To Damon? For T.J.'s sake?* Never! She jerked herself out of the family circle, her heartbeat loud in her head. "No! Damon and I are *not* getting married. T.J. is *not* Damon's child and we should not be having this discussion in front of him."

Soula nodded, but her black eyes were sharp with curiosity as she bit back her questions.

"Mummy, can I have a biscuit?" To Rebecca's relief T.J. seemed oblivious to the mood.

"Yes, of course, sweetie. Let me get you a napkin." Rebecca hurried to the sideboard, where a stack of paper napkins stood, her hands shaking as she reached out.

Damon got there first. "What does my mother mean?" he muttered, his back to Soula. "Who is T.J. the spitting image of?"

"Well, certainly not you," she huffed under her breath.

"Not unless he was born by immaculate conception." Damon's tone was barbed. Something flashed in his eyes. "So whose child is T.J.? My brother's?"

Rebecca turned away. Inside the ache grew and grew as the icy coldness expanded.

In a low voice that only she could hear he said, "My mother desperately wants a grandchild."

Shaking her head, desperate to escape him, Rebecca huddled into herself.

"Stop whispering, you two," Soula's voice broke in. "Rebecca's right—now's not the time. Rebecca, dear, I've poured you a cup of tea. Come sit next to me. Damon, do you want a cup?"

Rebecca shot Damon a despairing glance. His face was pale under his tan. A pulse beat violently in the hollow of his throat.

"Not for me, thank you," he replied grimly, making for the sliding doors. And Rebecca, holding the napkin, walked to where Soula sat with T.J. munching on the couch beside her.

There are things...things I haven't told you. Things you should've known...before we...before we slept together.

The damning words buzzed inside Damon's head, driving him mad. He stood alone on the wooden deck, staring blindly at the flat water of the lap pool. Behind him, from inside the house he could hear his mother's voice offering T.J. a short-bread biscuit, could hear Rebecca's cool, composed reply telling her son it was the last one. Blowing out hard, Damon swung around and slid the ranch slider closed to block out all sound of her.

But inside his head her words continued to echo. *There are things...things I haven't told you.* What had Rebecca meant? Was it possible...?

Yes, goddammit, it was possible! The boy could well have been fathered by Savvas. *His brother.* She'd dated his brother. Despite his orders that she stay away from Savvas.

She's a very beautiful woman. She was kind to me. We had some good times.

Savvas himself had admitted he'd been attracted to Rebecca. What man wouldn't be? His brother could easily be T.J.'s father. His mother had spotted the resemblance imme-diately. She'd taken one look at the boy's eyes and known he was an Asteriades.

How the hell had he missed it? Damon's knuckles whitened. Blood rushed in his ears. Hot, unsteady rage. He wanted to hit the wall. Anything. He restrained himself. He was losing it. That in itself was dangerous. He prided himself on his fierce, unrelenting control.

Yet he'd already lost every vestige of his control in passion. An image of Rebecca lying beneath him making hoarse little sounds as he drove into her welcoming body flashed in front of him, and he suppressed it ruthlessly. A tight, fist-curling anger threatened.

Rebecca…and Savvas.

God!

When had it happened? Another image, this time the memory of Savvas and Rebecca dancing at his wedding. Rebecca laughing up at Savvas. Had it happened on his wedding night? During his honeymoon? Was that when T.J. had been conceived? While he, Damon, was congratulating himself on finding the perfect bride? While he forced himself to be tender, to meet china-blue eyes, while he struggled to forget the unsuitable witch with slanted dark eyes? The curse of Rebecca—her devastating effect on the Asteriades men. His stomach turned.

Was this why she had agreed to come back to Auckland? Had money alone not been the only enticement? Or was it the hope of a fortune beyond her dreams, child support from Savvas Asteriades? No. He shook his head. That wasn't right. She'd had years to sue Savvas for child support. Yet she'd never claimed a cent. Why not? The money was legally due her, and she'd always been savvy when it came to money. So why had she walked away from the child maintenance claim?

He forced himself to take a deep breath. Trying to think right now was hard after the bombshell that had exploded in his face. Yes, he was furious with Rebecca. She hadn't told him the truth. But then, to be fair, when had he ever given her the opportunity?

There are things...things I haven't told you. The refrain whirled in his head. When had he ever indicated he'd listen calmly, rationally, to what she wanted discuss?

Hell, in the past he'd made it clear that he despised her. That would hardly have invited her to confide in him. Lately he'd had his own agenda: to court her, to get her into bed. Hardly a good time for her to confess that she'd borne his brother's child.

He raked hard fingers through his hair. T.J. was a great little kid. Angry as he was with Rebecca, he couldn't find it in himself to be angry that the kid existed. He only wished... Hell, he didn't want to think about that. *T.J. was not his son.*

But even though T.J. was his brother's child, there was no way in hell he intended to let Rebecca escape his grasp. He intended to keep her in his bed. He turned on his heel and reached for the handle on the ranch sliders. Through the glass he could see T.J. seated beside his mother, holding a cup. Rebecca stood beside them both.

What if Savvas broke off with Demetra when he found out about T.J.? What if Savvas decided that he wanted Rebecca *and* his son? He could not—would not—allow that to happen.

As the ranch sliders scraped open, Rebecca glanced up. His face must've given his state of mind away, because her expression grew apprehensive. She leaned forward, murmured something to his mother and disappeared out the opposite door.

Again anger surged in him. She was running away. But this time she would not escape.

Rebecca was his.

No matter who had fathered her child.

Eight

"**I** am correct, am I not?" Breathing hard, Damon caught up with Rebecca at her bedroom door. "T.J. is Savvas's child. That's what my mother saw, his resemblance to my brother. Isn't it?"

Rebecca tried to shut her bedroom door in Damon's angry face, but he stuck his foot into the gap and forced it open. Her hands clenched, her eyes smouldering in her unnaturally pale face, Rebecca stared at him, trying to think of something smart and cutting to say. But nothing came to mind.

Dammit. This was exactly why she'd retreated to her room with a feeble excuse to Soula that she needed a tissue. The last thing she wanted right now was a confrontation with Damon. She wanted a reprieve, time to think, to gather her defences. That scene downstairs had shattered her. Damon actually believed she'd slept with Savvas. It made her want to gag.

"Isn't it?" he repeated, coming closer. "Answer me, damn you!"

Outrage came off him in waves. She scuttled backward.

"Will you stop asking me about T.J.'s parentage. It has nothing, *nothing*, to do with you."

He followed her into the heart of the room. "Of course it does. It was Savvas! My brother was your lover. Savvas is T.J.'s father."

She edged back until the side of the bed pressed against the back of her knees. Trapped, she glared at him. "Savvas is *not* T.J.'s father."

"When was the child born?"

Now he wanted evidence? Absolutely fine. The pressure of the bed against the back of her knees increased. She resisted the urge to sit down.

"T.J." She paused meaningfully, "His name is T.J., remember?"

"Okay, when was T.J. born?"

Her heart pounding, she told him. And then told herself it didn't matter. There were no inferences he could draw because T.J. had been a couple of weeks premature—although the obstetrician had said it was no cause to worry, joking that if he hadn't known better, he would have sworn T.J. was *overdue* by a couple of weeks.

"Don't play me for a fool. I can add. It all fits together. You dated my brother after my wedding, had his baby and kept it from him...and from me. What kind of woman are you?"

She wanted to scream, to pound her fists against his chest. *How could he get it all so wrong?* Instead she counted to five, then spoke in a slow voice, the way she did when T.J. was being particularly contrary. "You're jumping to conclusions—"

"So what else is there? That you were sleeping with other—"

"No!" She put her hands over her ears and bowed her head.

Damon grasped her arms and pulled them away from her face. He wanted to see her eyes. "Listen to me." This time Rebecca was going to listen to him, she wasn't going to block him out. This close he could feel the soft, moist breath from her ragged breaths, smell the exotic, feminine scent of her body.

Her wrists were slim in his large hands. With a sense of shock he became aware of her fragility, how much stronger he was. Strange, because she'd always challenged him, never given an inch, so he'd never been aware that this more delicate side of her existed. The last time he'd been this close to her, last night, he'd been so overwhelmed by forbidden emotions, so busy fighting a losing battle. Making love to her…

"No." With one sharp movement she twisted her wrists out his grasp.

She was hotly furious, he realised and drew a deep, calming breath. "Rebecca, I could not let my mother discover the truth. It might upset her. In her medical state, it could trigger a heart attack. It could even kill her."

"Truth?" She laughed, a hard, angry sound. "You wouldn't recognise the truth if it hit you in a bar fight."

"I prefer not to brawl in bars," he said with a calmness he was far from feeling.

Rebecca looked mad enough to hit him. No hint of fragility remained. With her fisted hands, her chin pushed pugnaciously forward and her long hair dishevelled, she looked beautiful. Desire twisted inside him. Even now he wanted her.

She uncurled her fingers, sighed and pushed her hair behind her ears. "I wish I'd never come back, never gotten involved with you. I know I'm not blameless." She paused, looking oddly hesitant after her burst of fury. She opened her mouth. "Look, I owe you an—"

"Tell me," he cut across her, unaccountably hurt by the words she'd thrown at him. "What are you going to tell Savvas? What do you think this will do to Demetra?"

"Listen to me, Damon. I like Demetra, dammit!"

"You claimed to love Felicity like a sister. She was your best friend, yet you did your damnedest to break us up."

"Because I knew you were wrong for each other. Because I thought she—"

He snorted. "Because you thought you were right for me?"

"No! Yes. Oh—"

"See? You can't even answer a simple question truthfully."

She flinched, the last colour draining from her lily-white skin until she looked waxen. And just like that the fragility, her vulnerability, knocked the heart out of Damon's anger and frustration, leaving remorse in the vacuum that remained. With shock he realised that he was in danger of becoming twisted around her long, elegant fingers. Panic ignited in his brain, scattering his thoughts. He was no different from her wretched husband.

He gulped in air and rallied what remained of his tattered shreds of sense together, but the alarm and fear refused to go. "After last night was I supposed to fall for your tricks? Declare undying love, like Grainger—"

"Leave Aaron out of this! You know nothing—"

"That's what you keep telling me—I know nothing. Nothing about Felicity. Nothing about Grainger. Nothing about you. But, you forget, I *do* know you." He pressed his body up against hers, vividly aware of the bed that waited behind her. She was soft against him, her lush breasts full against his chest. He inhaled sharply. Her scent was fresh and incredibly sexy. He nudged closer still. Resenting her. But turned on, too.

"Stop it, damn you."

"Make me." He wedged a thigh between hers, intensely conscious of the brevity of her shorts, the softness of her bare legs. He was breathing hard. "No more winding me around your little finger—"

A broken laugh escaped her. "You? Around *my* little finger?"

"Yes," he murmured, caught in her spell. "That's what you do, isn't it? Isn't it?" He pressed his hips up against hers.

She toppled onto the bed with a cry.

He dropped down beside her.

He intended to kiss her. A hard kiss. A punishing kiss for making him want her this much, for confusing him, for turning his life inside out.

But that was before he read the stark bewilderment in her eyes. This close the hurt in her dark, slanting eyes dominated his vision. They seemed to drill down into his heart. God knew what she saw there. The thought killed all desire stone cold. Instead he felt weary, tired and very uncertain.

Yet under the exhaustion, the confusion, he desperately wanted to salvage something. He didn't want to lose her. Not again. Not when he'd only just found her.

"So what happens now?" he asked.

"God!" There was annoyance in her voice. "You are such a bastard."

He tried to smile. "Don't say that to my mother."

"This is not funny, damn you."

"No, it's not." At once it all came rushing back. *Rebecca. Savvas. T.J.* With a sigh he sat up, slung his legs over the edge of the bed and dropped his head in his hands. "What a mess!"

Frustration closed around him like a suffocating red mist. He fought it. He banged a fist on the bedside table. The lamp rattled. Her purse slid off, fell with a thud onto the floor. Behind him he heard her breath catch.

He turned. Her eyes were wide.

Remorse filled him. "Rebecca, I would never hurt you—"

"I know that." She blew out hard. "The sound gave me a fright."

He knew it was more than that. She was on edge. And he wasn't helping matters. He was losing control, frightening her. Frightening himself. A sigh tore from his throat. "I'm sorry."

"It's okay."

Her eyes were velvety again. She'd forgiven him. Their eyes held. Her tongue tip appeared. Pink. Provocative. It flicked across her bottom lip. His heart started to pound. Without thinking, he bent toward her. Her breathing quickened. She wasn't going to rebuff him. Much as he probably deserved it.

Then her eyes glazed over and the pink tongue disappeared. "Damon, this is not a good idea. We need to talk."

She was right. They needed to talk. And he needed to pull himself together; he was too far under her spell for his peace of mind. Damon pulled away, stood and bent to pick up the purse he'd knocked off the bedstand. It had fallen open. Inside a photo of a handsome dark-haired man confronted Damon. The stranger faced the camera, his hands tucked into the pockets of faded jeans; he wore a reckless smile and the devil glinted in his eye.

"So who is he?" He held up her purse. "Another foolish lover?"

"Stop it!"

"Why? We both know how attractive you are to my sex."

Rebecca simply looked confused.

"Oh, please." He'd been aware of her ripe, taunting sensuality the first time they had met. Was it possible that she had no idea of the sexuality she projected? She had to be aware of it. Or perhaps not. He sighed. "Perhaps you don't deliberately lure them to you, perhaps it is just the unusual chemistry of beauty and that subtle challenge your very existence offers."

"So I'm no longer a little scheming bitch then?"

He paused, detecting hurt, a hint of aggression as if he'd wronged her in some way. He'd never called her that. Or had he? He tilted his head, trying to remember. "Let's just say you're not slow to take advantage of the qualities nature endowed you with."

She glared at him from the bed.

"But you haven't answered my question. Who the hell is he?" The burning curiosity astounded him. Damon wanted to find the stranger, tear him to pieces. How dare she carry another man's photo in her purse when she made love to him like a wicked angel? "What's his name?"

"James."

"And where is he now?" he was driven to ask.

"Dead."

The answer jolted him. Rebecca no longer glared at him.

Her face wore a faraway expression, remote, and her eye
were lifeless. He wanted to shake her, kiss her, tell her to focu
on him, that he lived.

"I'm sorry." But he wasn't at all sorry that the man she'
cared for was dead. He didn't need that kind of competition
And then he realised what he'd thought....

Competition. He stalked to the window and stared blindl
into the falling dusk. When had it all become a competition
When had it become so important that Rebecca's attention b
taken up with him and only him?

And why did anyone else matter? He had her now. Wha
did James…Aaron…even Savvas matter? Now there was onl
him. And he had no intention of letting her forget that.

"Forget James." He swung back. In two long strides he wa
back on the bed beside her. He pushed her flat and followe
her down. He didn't dare name the dark, hot emotion tha
coursed through him, making him determined to eradicate th
memory of the other man, this James.

He kissed her with dark, sexual purpose. She jerked as hi
mouth took hers. His mouth softened at once. And it all change
She gave a mewing groan and responded. No holds barred.

There!

Fierce triumph filled him. He reared up and stared int
her aroused face, flushed with passion. "Did James kiss yo
like that? Did you feel that same wild abandonment that yo
feel with me?"

"Get away from me!"

"Admit it's good." He leaned to kiss her again. She pun
melled his chest.

"Get off me."

He let her go and sat up. "Oh, for heaven's sake!" Her re
top had ridden up, revealing the creamy skin of her midrif
He forced his gaze away before his thoughts scattered. "H
couldn't have meant anything to yo—"

"Why? Because I devour men like some black widow

Twist them around my little finger like trophies in some cruel game? Because I'm incapable of love?"

"Hell." He couldn't meet the reproachful challenge in her gaze. Something tugged inside him at the thought of her loving this James. He didn't want her loving anyone...except him, he realised bleakly. He wanted her to save all that passion, all her smouldering ardour, for him and him alone. No man should mean anything to her, not while she made love with him with such sweetness.

He was jealous.

But before he could examine how in God's name that had happened, he saw the tears spill onto her cheeks, and his heart tightened.

Rebecca who never cried.

Who had now cried twice in as many days.

Rebecca who gave as good as she got was sobbing her heart out...

She had loved this man, this James.

The realisation devastated him. He turned away, needing to think about how he was going to deal with this latest discovery.

"I'm sorry," he repeated. This time it was true. He didn't want to see her pain.

"Why? Because I loved someone? Or are you sorry for James? Maybe I drove him to suicide, too? Is that what you believe?"

He flinched at the acid words.

"Well, let me tell you this. He didn't commit suicide. James was ill, terminally ill. But the funny thing is that he died in a car accident. A merciful release, everyone told me. But you know what? It doesn't make it any easier. I miss him." And she started to cry again, great wrenching sobs that make his heart tear.

"Shh." Damon was beside her in a flash. Pulling her into his arms, he leaned back against the padded headboard, cradling her.

"Aaron, James—both dead."

She sounded utterly desolate.

"Hush," he repeated, at a loss of how to resolve this. How could it be that a wealthy man, a man responsible for the livelihoods of thousands, a man who prided himself on his control and who was admired as a business leader, a negotiator, a solution maker, didn't know how to deal with the grief of the woman in his arms?

"Aaron, then James and then Fliss, too. Everyone I love dies." She shuddered. His body vibrated with the force of it. "Yesterday T.J. nearly died, too."

She wanted him to believe she'd loved Aaron? And James? Perhaps in her own fashion she had. And what about Savvas? Perhaps she wasn't a woman who could only have one great love, as his mother had.

He tried to tell himself none of it mattered. But it did. It mattered very much. He desired her—wanted her with an endless yearning—even if he had to slay the shadows of a whole slew of ghosts in her past. Rebecca was the woman she was today precisely because of the relationships that had shaped her. Relationships with other men. They were part of her. If he wanted to keep her, he'd have to live with that, accept it, or he'd have no peace. He'd be torn apart every time he held her, made love to her.

She was still weeping, great tearing sobs that pierced him to the soul. He held her tightly. Tried to think of something to say that might help her deal with the loss of this…James. The loss of her husband.

Suddenly he found it. "When my father died, I was furious with him for leaving us so suddenly. It hurt so much, too. I didn't know what was worse—the pain or the rage." It was true. He'd felt deserted by his father. The father who'd been like a god to him. All-powerful. Above death. Damon stroked Rebecca's hair. "But the pain passes. And for you it will, too. You're strong, the strongest woman I've ever known."

This time it was Rebecca who pulled away. He tried to hold her, but she wriggled until she'd put distance between them. Turning, she met his gaze, and he flinched at the bleak despair he saw there.

"James wasn't my lover. He was my brother."

The revelation struck him like a blow. His breath caught. "I didn't know you had a brother." But instantly the pressure that had been building inside him deflated.

James was not her lover.

"We were put in foster care but not together, not since I was ten. But we kept in touch. James grew wild, a real rebel. He went off the tracks for a while. Then later there was a girl…"

"There always is," he said wryly.

"They fell in love. But she was scared, scared of the wildness in him. Insecurity and fear drove her away. James was devastated. He pulled himself together. They found each other. But then…he felt ill, tired. We thought he had the flu." She fell silent and shot him an odd glance. Then she swallowed. "James was diagnosed with cancer."

Damon had a funny feeling that hadn't been what she had been about to say. But he wasn't about to challenge her, not now. Not while her renewed pain was so fresh.

"Come. Let me hold you."

She snuggled against him. "This is so weird. All my life I'd been the strong one. The rock Fliss clung to, the person who fought to get James help, the one who held them when they cried, hugged them when they got lonely. But there was no one to hug me."

"What about Felicity?"

She shrugged. "Fliss was needy. I'm not going to say more. I loved her. She loved me."

"But she was draining, too," he said slowly.

"Yes."

"What about James—he was your brother. Didn't he look after you?"

She sighed. "I told you, we were separated. And he got in with the wrong crowd."

Damon shook his head, wishing he was hearing something different.

"Drugs." Rebecca sighed. "He got into drugs. He was in a downward spiral."

"So he was needy, too."

"Kind of. But his foster parents had a younger teen. They didn't want him influenced by James."

"And so…?" he prompted.

"I convinced his foster parents to get him help. It took two years, quite a bit of money—some of which I had to pay—and he cleaned up his act. I was working by then, for Aaron."

She stared past him with unseeing eyes, the sorrow reflecting only the ghosts of the past. Damon's throat tightened. He pressed a kiss meant to comfort on top of her head.

"So that's how you met."

She nodded. "He asked me out. I said no. After all, what would a wealthy guy like him want with me except for the obvious? I was young, not stupid."

Damon couldn't believe she'd placed such a low value on herself. But given her upbringing, he imagined her self-esteem would have been rock-bottom. "No, never only that. Aaron Grainger was a wise man." Far wiser than he had been. "He saw a woman who was intelligent, funny, smart."

She looked up at him, doubt in her face. "You think so?"

"I know so." He swallowed. "Now tell me about Grainger."

"Aaron wouldn't take no for an answer. He kept asking."

Of course Grainger had kept asking—she was beautiful…and young. How young? he wondered. "How old were you?"

"Eighteen."

Eighteen. Grainger deserved to be shot; he'd been at least fifteen years older. "And then…?"

"Fliss wanted to become a chef. She'd done a couple of local cooking courses, but she wanted to train in France. And

James was in trouble again—this was before he got his life back together."

Damon closed his eyes, suspecting what was coming. He remembered how proud he'd been of his wife's talents, her Cordon Bleu skills. Never had he realised how they'd been financed. And he'd had the gall to tell Rebecca on one occasion that she should take a leaf out of Fliss's book, to stop trying to be the world's greatest entrepreneur and get some skills. As Fliss had.

God, how arrogant he'd been!

He wished he could take every thoughtless, cruel comment back.

Rebecca hadn't uttered a word in her own defence. Hadn't pointed out she'd been getting things done while those around her clung to her for support. He couldn't help wondering what else she'd failed to tell him.

"Okay, so you asked Grainger for the money to pay for all that, and he demanded you marry him in return," he said flatly and he held her tight in his arms.

"No, no." She gave him another of those strange, unfathomable looks. "I asked Aaron for a loan to pay for Fliss's plane ticket and Cordon Bleu course. I found a fabulous therapist for James to see. Aaron was fantastic, refused to accept interest on the loan, said I worked hard. I started staying later each day to make up for the interest-free bit. He insisted on taking me to dinner a couple of times. I discovered I liked him."

"I'm sure you did." Damon remembered how personable Grainger had been and found himself resenting the manipulation the other man had used. What eighteen-year-old could have resisted that? Let alone one who was starved of attention. Rebecca would've had no social life, only debt to work off. She'd have been a pushover.

"It was so nice to have someone else to lean on for a change. I told him about my dream. I wanted to be independent. One day I wanted to start a business of my own. He encouraged me, offered me a loan."

"Interest-free again?" Damon found he couldn't keep the edge out of his voice.

"No, this time the loan was done through the bank. But he arranged me a good deal with a low interest rate. The day I left his employ and started Dream Occasions he took me out to dinner, ordered champagne—the real French stuff—told me he'd already referred me to a whole lot of friends and colleagues." She smiled. "I was a little horrified. Then he told me he loved me and asked me if I would marry him."

She had felt obligated! The man had played Svengali to her Trilby.

"You didn't have to marry him."

"I know. But I was nineteen by then." She shrugged, matter-of-fact. "What do you know at nineteen? I'd always wanted security and Aaron handed it to me. I thought my dreams had come true. It all happened so fast."

And just as fast she'd been the manhunter of the year, snaring one of Auckland's most elusive bachelors, establishing a successful business.

The piranhas had been circling.

"There were rumours," he said slowly.

"About my lover? The drug addict? That was James."

It made sense.

"And the others?"

"Others?"

"The other lovers?"

She stared at him, her dark eyes flat and unfathomable. "What about them?"

"Tell me about them." His chest contracted at his demand.

Her face had lost all animation. "I've told you before. I don't kiss and tell."

"But what about my brother?" Pain like a knife twisted in Damon's chest. "Surely I deserve to know about him?"

She struggled out of his arms. "I told you—he never was

my lover." Rebecca sat on the edge of the bed, her back to him, her hands hanging loose between her knees.

Damn, he didn't want her so far away. He wanted her back in his arms. "When? When did you me tell that?"

She turned to look at him. "When you threw it at me that he was T.J.'s father."

"No," he said slowly, trying to remember back to the exact words she'd used. "You denied that he was T.J.'s father—you never denied sleeping with him."

"Oh."

He could see her thinking about it, myriad thoughts crossing her delicate face.

"Well, I haven't," she said finally.

Could he trust her on this?

His heart wanted to. Straightening, Damon caught her chin in his hand and searched her eyes. They were dark, filled with secrets. But she met his gaze without flinching. At last he released her chin.

"You believe me?"

He did. No, he was confused. Hell, he didn't know what to think anymore.

And there was still the boy. "So who the devil is T.J.'s father?"

"Does it matter?"

Her secrets ate at him. She consumed him. He wanted to know everything about her. Of course it mattered! "I don't want to one day walk into a room and be faced with the man who fathered your child. Not without warning."

"Trust me," she said. "That will never happen."

Trust her.

Trust her? Just like that?

Damon couldn't believe how badly he wanted to do just that. It was curiously liberating.

Nine

"Okay." Rebecca drew a deep, shuddering breath. "Look, maybe it's time to tell you something else about T.J. Something I've waited too long to tell you. But I was afraid—" She broke off.

"Afraid?" Damon prompted, coming closer.

Rebecca forced herself to continue, not to run a million miles away. She stared at the strong features she loved so much. "Not long ago you said I'm the strongest woman you've ever known. But I must be the most fearful, too."

He brushed a strand of hair from her face. "So tell me," he invited. "What are you afraid of?"

Damon was so confident, so sure of himself. Why had she ever thought that the truth she'd hidden so carefully might hurt him? "Well, there are lots of things. I'm afraid of losing those I love. You know that."

His gaze softened. Wordlessly he covered her hand with his. His touch was warm and comforting. It gave her the courage to carry on. She took a deep breath. "I'm afraid of hurting people, most of all I'm afraid of hurting you."

"Don't worry about that. You couldn't hurt me. I'm tough." But his eyes turned a shade darker as wariness crept in. "So why don't you just spit out this big dark secret of yours?"

"Okay." She squeezed her eyes shut, murmured a prayer and clutched his hand like a lifeline. "T.J. is Fliss's son. Not mine. I adopted him."

The silence was total.

Nothing moved. But his hand grew stiff in hers. Rebecca opened her eyes.

Damon dropped her hand and rose slowly to his feet, his face white. Finally his mouth moved. "T.J. is my son?"

"No."

"I heard you, Rebecca," Damon accused. Every last vestige of humour had fled. "You said he was Fliss's son. You kept this from me?"

"I—"

"You what exactly?"

"I wanted to tell you that he's Fliss's son."

"When?"

"I was trying to tell you…" She drew a quick, fortifying breath. "I wanted to tell you before—"

Before we made love. But she couldn't speak of love. Not while he stood there so pale and angry. Rebecca shut her eyes in frustration.

"You—" He broke off. She flinched and opened her eyes, waiting for the invective to follow. "You robbed me of my son."

"Stop it!" she yelled. "T.J. is not your son."

"What?" The bones of his face stood out sharply under his tan. "What do you mean he's not my son?" He was grappling, searching for words. "But I heard you…you said he was Fliss's son." But the massive self-confidence had dwindled. He looked shaken.

"I didn't want to ever have to tell you this."

"Tell me what?"

"Fliss…" Her voice trailed off.

"What? What about Felicity? Talk, dammit."

"Fliss was in love with my brother. He asked her to marry him."

"James." His voice was colourless. "Your brother. He'd recovered from his addiction, hadn't he? So why the hell didn't she marry him if everything was so damned perfect in Eden?"

"Because she was insecure. You have to understand. Fliss lost her parents when she was nine. She was terrified of change. She wanted security above all else. James's cancer horrified her. She couldn't stand beside him and watch him die. And then she met you."

He folded his arms, closing himself off from her. "You're telling me I was her meal ticket?"

"Oh, no, no. It went much deeper than that. You're more than simply a rich billionaire." Was she getting through to him? Or was she wasting her time? "You're strong, confident, respected. Fliss craved all that. Nothing was ever going to go wrong with you around."

"But it did. She left me after barely six weeks of marriage. Without a word of explanation she upped and left with you. No sooner was the honeymoon over and the bride fled."

He'd hated that, Rebecca realised. He must have thought himself the laughingstock of the city.

He was glaring down at her now. "Did you and Fliss laugh yourselves silly when you read the papers? Did you see what they said about me? They wondered what kind of monster I turned into after dark."

"No," she said slowly. "I didn't know. We didn't read the papers. James…the cancer was spreading. Losing Fliss had jolted him. He'd decided to try radiation. I came to tell Fliss. The only reason Fliss left you was because James wanted to see her before the radiation. He was terrified of the treatment. I think Fliss grew up very quickly right then. She couldn't bury her head in the sand anymore. He loved her, he needed her."

Damon had grown fuzzy in front of her. The whole room blurred. Rebecca blinked. A hot tear splashed down her cheek. Impatiently she smeared it away.

"And she went?"

"Yes. I only meant her to go for a day. James was here, in Auckland, for a final consultation before the treatment started. But once she saw him—" Rebecca broke off. How could she explain how Fliss had felt?

Fliss had felt terrible about abandoning James, about betraying him by marrying another man while she still loved him. There'd been guilt, too, that she hadn't stood by James while he came to terms with his diagnosis. Fliss had faced the fact that she could no longer run, that she wanted to spend whatever time he had left at his side. Yes, James had cancer, but there was a slim chance that he might survive. This time she'd chosen to betray Damon and her marriage vows.

"In the days before the treatment she stayed with James in my apartment. After the radiation—" Rebecca swallowed "—they discovered she was pregnant. It was like a miracle."

"But she was still *my* wife," Damon growled.

"That was the only thing that put a damper on their happiness. They'd have to wait the legally required two years before Fliss could divorce you. James was scared he'd be dead by then. So they decided to live each day to the fullest. James was convinced the baby was a sign that he would make it. But six months later the cancer was back. This time the doctors weren't as optimistic. But James and Fliss wouldn't accept it. They thought James would pull through."

Except they had both died. James had been having a good week. The baby was due soon. He'd agreed to attend a party in his honour, celebrating his temporary reprieve and their baby's imminent birth. Fliss had been blooming and James had so desperately wanted to live. For Fliss. For the baby.

No one had foreseen a car accident. James had been killed instantly. Fliss had held on long enough to speak to Rebecca, to sign a will and an application for a birth certificate…to hold her baby and name him Tyler James. There had been a lot of blood loss, shock, multiple transfusions before she passed away.

Rebecca had walked away with a huge lump of a bruise where the seat belt had restrained her and a massive case of survivor's guilt.

She started when Damon put his hands on her shoulders.

"And while she was pursuing her future happiness with your brother, she didn't think to tell me why she'd left? To call? She owed me an explanation."

She shrugged his hands away and stood. "Your wife was scared you'd be angry. She thought you'd come after her—she planned to tell you then."

"I don't think so," he drawled. "I suspect she hoped you would explain it all for her when I finally turned up. Except I didn't."

"No, you served her with a separation agreement instead and washed your hands of her."

"And gave her a healthy payoff. What happened to that?"

Rebecca raised her chin as a wave of anger swept her. "It formed part of Fliss's estate. I invested it for T.J. He'll get it when he turns twenty-five. Sue him then."

"Laws of prescription aside, I wouldn't do that to the boy. I don't need that money." He considered her, his head tipped to one side, inspecting her as though she were an unfamiliar species. "What really interests me is why Felicity thought she could marry me while she loved someone else."

Rebecca sighed. "I've wondered that myself too many times to count. She didn't think she and James would work out. Not with James refusing even to talk about his cancer, refusing to discuss radiation and pretending it didn't exist. Fliss was terrified of being abandoned after his death, I think. I honestly believe she hoped she'd grow to love you." Rebecca had clung to that hope. That Damon and Fliss's marriage would work. Only that would make the pain she'd suffered worth it.

"And you?" He was curious, she saw. "What did you think about all this?"

She glanced away. "It wasn't my decision to make."

"But you didn't approve."

It was a statement, not a question. Surprised, she stared at him. He'd anticipated her reaction. "No. I told her she shouldn't marry you."

"You told me that, too." His mouth twisted. "What else did you tell her?"

"That it wasn't fair on you, that she was cheating you. But I couldn't tell you that. Her relationship with my brother wasn't my secret. So I tried to convince her that both of you would suffer if she didn't break it off." Did he finally believe her? It was hard to gauge.

"Pity that neither of us took your advice. Arrogant fool that I was, I thought your motives were suspect. Quite simply I thought you wanted me for yourself. How utterly conceited. I should've noticed that the moment I started courting Felicity you never once flirted with me again."

"Not quite true." She gave him a sad smile. "Remember the rehearsal, the night before the wedding?"

"When you begged me not to marry Fliss, told me she'd regret it? And when I refused to listen, you threw yourself at me, kissed me. How could I ever forget?"

It had been a life-defining moment for her. She'd told Damon that he couldn't marry Fliss. He'd stared at her down his impressive nose without deigning to respond, looking at her as if she were trash. Something inside her had snapped. The next thing she knew, her arms had been wrapped around his neck, her body plastered against his. She'd stared at his beautiful, sensuous mouth. Then she'd kissed him. Open-mouthed, with all the passion she could muster. She'd put everything she felt for him into that kiss.

"You did kiss me back," she said at last.

"Ah, God, how could I not? You were pure sin, pure delight. I couldn't stop myself. I should have seen sense then. Instead I thought I'd gone mad, tempted by a woman—"

"You despised."

"Yes," he said very quietly. "But I lied to myself. Self-preservation. You terrified me."

"So you pushed me away and told me never to come near Fliss again after the wedding."

"I seem to remember I called you some vile names. Some of the anger you bore the brunt of was directed at myself. I couldn't believe I'd kissed you back, that I'd been weak enough to betray Fliss. I'd always considered myself a man of principle."

And for a heart-stopping second Rebecca wondered if he'd ever be able to forgive himself for that breach of honour. He'd hated the passion, the emotion she aroused in him. Now she could see his abhorrence for what he considered his weakness of character. Would that reckless kiss the night before his wedding come between them now, almost four years later, and drive them apart?

"You were arrogant. She was my best friend and I knew she would do whatever you wanted. I felt betrayed by both of you. You broke my heart. So I flirted with you shamelessly on the dance floor the next day."

His face became sombre. "I'd wounded you, called you names, treated you like dirt. I deserved everything you dished out. But my question still stands. Apart from those two occasions, you never flirted with me after Fliss and I started to date. Nor were you ever hostile to her." He paused. "Why was that?"

"I can't say I didn't hope that Fliss would come to her senses and remember James. Fliss was like a sister to me. I loved her. My brother loved her, too. How could I hate her or flirt with the man who was interested in her?"

"Even though she snaffled the man you desired? She did it under false pretences, yet you still loved her?"

"Yes, I still loved her." Rebecca met his frowning gaze squarely. "Even though she married you when she should've known better."

"I admire your loyalty. It's a pity Felicity didn't show you the same loyalty."

"I don't think she realised...quite what I felt for you." It was painful to admit.

Damon looked disbelieving.

Rebecca flushed. "I was painfully obvious, wasn't I? Must've been very amusing to you. But I'd never felt that kind of...response to any man. After Aaron, I never thought I'd marry again. Then *poof*—" she snapped her fingers "—there was this out-of-control yearning." Her voice shook. "You and me, I thought it was meant to be."

"I'm sorry." He touched her cheek. "I was cruel."

"Yes." She ducked her head away.

His hand fell to his side. "I judged you."

"Yes."

"You didn't defend yourself."

"If it had been meant to be, I wouldn't have needed to defend myself."

A silence followed her words.

He'd turned white under his tan again. "I deserved that. I listened to the rumour mongering of fools. I heard only what I wanted—" He broke off.

"I wasn't prepared to stoop to counter the rumours." Rebecca held her head high. "Some of them tried it on with me—"

"And you told them to go to hell?"

"Something like that."

"So they destroyed your reputation."

"More like they didn't want the rest of the boys to think they were the only ones who didn't get lucky." Her mouth twisted. "The stories of my...accomplishments...grew in the telling."

"God!" He raked fingers through his long hair, pushing i back. "A lot has happened in the past couple of days…today There's a lot I need to think about, Rebecca. I need time."

She bit her lip. Here it was—the kiss of death. She'd known that what they had now would not survive the long shadov of the past.

"Do you want me and T.J. to go?"

"No." His blue eyes looked weary. "No. Never that. But need time to think this through. I've discovered that a lot o what I believed is false, I've learned some things that hav made me not particularly like myself. I need time to come t terms with it all."

This was all because of his twisted sense of honour. H couldn't forgive himself for kissing her when he'd pledge himself to another. He couldn't forgive himself for the hu he'd caused her. All because of what he saw as his ow weakness. Every time he looked at her he'd remember hov he'd failed himself.

And what was the point of arguing? He said he wante time. Rebecca suspected he wanted to inveigle himself out c a dead-end situation. Because of the past, they had no future What future was there with a woman who every day of hi life would remind him of the humiliation of the past? So wha if he desired her—had even come to like her? There was n point in fooling herself that he'd ever love her the way sh wanted to be loved.

Rebecca raised her chin. "I understand."

"I don't think you do." He gave a sigh of frustration. "Look I'm flying—"

"Rebecca, we're home." Demetra's voice floated throug the house.

Damon swore.

A moment later the door burst open. "Oops, sorry Demetra's hand flew to her mouth.

Damon snarled something in Greek, leaped from the be

and barged out the room, leaving Demetra staring wide-eyed at Rebecca.

"Wow. What did I interrupt? What have I missed? Tell me everything!"

Rebecca had just watched T.J. drift off to sleep when a knock sounded on her bedroom door. She hurried across before the sound could rouse T.J. and yanked the door open.

Damon stood there, his knuckles poised to rap again, his eyes guarded. "I came to say goodbye."

For an instant her heart stopped and she felt winded.

He must have seen the shock in her eyes, because he pushed his hands into his hair. "I'm leaving to go to L.A. tomorrow, remember? For two weeks?"

The business trip. Of course. Why had she been so shaken? Perhaps because "goodbye" was her worse nightmare? Because he'd said he needed time, and deep down she feared that meant it was over? "Come in." Rebecca stood aside.

Something—desire?—flashed in Damon's eyes. But he didn't move. "No, I'm not coming in. I wanted to give you a cheque."

Rebecca frowned. "A cheque? For what?"

"For the time and work you've spent on the wedding so far—to tide you over until I get back."

"I can't take it." She backed away from the cheque he was thrusting at her.

"Don't be ridiculous. You've earned it. That's why you came back to Auckland originally. Take it."

"That's *not* why I came back to Auckland." Her heart tore and her temper snapped. "You are so blind!"

His head snapped back. "Okay, so why did you agree to do the wedding then?"

She looked away. "Because your mother was sick and you were worried about her." Her voice was low, even to her own ears.

"Spare me! I can't talk now." He thrust it at her and started to walk away.

Without looking at the face of the cheque, she tore it across. "I can't accept it. It's in breach of my contract."

That stopped him in his tracks. He swung around, his eyes narrow slits in that barbarian face. "What contract?"

"The contract selling Dream Occasions. I have a restraining clause."

"But you sold the business nearly four years ago. It would be unreasonable that you couldn't work as a wedding planner in the city after two years."

"I had a clause restraining me from contacting old clients for five years. That's not up yet."

"My mother was never your client."

"But you were."

And she saw the memory hit him. When he'd thrown the cheque at her the night before his wedding to Fliss, told her to take it as payment for the work she'd done for him and Fliss. Defiantly she'd taken it, holding the gaze that was full of contempt. At first she'd kept it as a reminder of her stupidity for falling for a man who hated her.

And later, when he'd served the separation agreement on Fliss, she'd endorsed the cheque and given it to Fliss. When Fliss died, the proceeds of Fliss's estate together with the payout from Fliss's life insurance policy had all been invested. T.J. would inherit a tidy sum when he was twenty-five.

"So, I'm sorry, I can't accept that payment." She held Damon's narrowed gaze, refusing to drop her own.

"Why?"

She pretended to misunderstand him. "I told you—the contract."

"No." He made an impatient gesture. "Why did you agree to help with the wedding?"

She gave a little huff of impatience. "Don't you listen to anything I say? I told you that, too. Because your mother was ill. And you were worried about her. How could I turn my back on you both then? When you were suffering? How could I walk away when your mother might be dying?"

He flinched. "It was the one thing guaranteed to change your mind, wasn't it? After all the losses you have suffered, you couldn't leave me to face the chance that my mother might die alone. And I never even realised. Stupid!" He banged his palm against his forehead. "But you should still have told me you couldn't accept payment."

"I did. I kept repeating it. But you wouldn't listen!"

"I thought that you agreed to do the wedding because I doubled my offer. I thought it was the money. And when you told me your mother had deserted you and James, that you didn't know who your father was, I started to understand why you were driven to be so self-sufficient. I realised why money is so important to you and for the first time it stopped maddening me that I'd had to pay you a damned fortune to get you back to Auckland. But, as usual, I screwed up." His eyes were a dark, pained blue. "I don't know anything about what goes on in that beautiful head, do I? God, what a mess." He sank his hands into his face. When he finally raised his head, Damon looked haggard. "It never changes, does it?"

"It really doesn't matter," she said.

Damon watched her with an expression she could not read. The silence was unnerving. At last he exhaled and said flatly, "It matters." Then he turned on his heel and walked away.

The knowledge that Damon had jetted out to L.A. made the house feel as if the heart had been ripped out. Rebecca found it hard to settle down on Monday morning to make the calls she needed to. Nothing filled the hollowness within her. Finally she made a deal with herself. She would go back to Tohunga for a few days, maybe a week. But only after she'd completed the list of tasks she'd set herself for the week— that would give her a goal. And she'd start with finalising the seating arrangements for the wedding with Soula, which Demetra—typically—wanted no part in.

She found Soula in the lounge.

"Rebecca, *pethi*, don't hover in the doorway. Come sit down. I've been wanting to speak to you, child." Soula set aside the piece of tapestry she'd been working on. "Has T.J. gone with Demetra?"

Rebecca nodded. "He loves helping Demetra. Personally I think it's the joy of making mud. But today is a special treat. T.J.'s going to watch the landscapers transplanting giant full-grown palms into Demetra's front garden. He can't wait to see the crane."

"We must be grateful. He's recovered well from a nasty experience."

Rebecca crossed the room and sank down beside Soula. "Dr. Campbell told me it would take a while before he feels completely secure, that he'll need a lot of attention and love until he comes to terms with it." Rebecca hesitated. "Soula, there is something I need to tell you."

Oh, where to begin? Rebecca fidgeted with her fingers.

"What is it, *pethi?*" Soula's eyes were sombre. "Ah, don't tell me you can't arrange Savvas and Demetra's wedding? That you are leaving?"

How had Soula known?

Rebecca looked up. "I need a break for a few days. I want to go to Tohunga and check that everything is okay with my business and my house. But, don't worry, I will be back to finish arranging the wedding."

"Pah." Soula flapped an arm. "I'm not worried about the wedding. I'm more worried that once you leave you may never return."

"I'll be back," Rebecca promised.

"When will you go?"

"I thought I'd leave at noon on Friday. That way I can reach Tohunga by late afternoon."

Soula slid her a sideways look. "Does Damon know about this?"

She shook her head. "But he's going to be away for two weeks. I'm only going for a week—I'll be back by the time he returns."

Soula gave an impatient puff. "Well, what can I say? If you need to check on your business, then you must do so, my child. Now tell me about T.J."

"T.J.?" Rebecca could feel the blood draining from her face. "What do you want to know?"

"When do you intend to tell me that he is not your son?"

"Is it so obvious?" Shaken, she stared at Damon's mother. "How did you know?"

"Oh, Rebecca, Rebecca." Soula shook her head sadly. "Except for the dark hair and the eyes, he is the spitting image of Fliss. The curls, the heart-shaped face, the dimples are all Fliss."

She'd already had this discussion with Damon. It was good to have it all out in the open. She was so tired of living a lie.

"So why did you pretend yesterday that you thought he was *my* son? Mine and Damon's?"

"I wanted to give that son of mine a shove in a direction he should have taken a long time ago." Soula gave a weak but wicked smile. "That way everything works out. You keep T.J., whom you obviously adore, and T.J. gets to have the love of a mother and his blood father."

"Wait a moment." This was going to be hard. But she'd committed to the truth, so there was no other way. Rebecca picked her words carefully. "Soula, T.J. is not Damon's son."

"Of course he is. He has the Asteriades eyes."

"No, those are Fliss's eyes—"

"Yes, they are blue, and I grant that they are the same shape as his mother's. But the colour is pure Asteriades. My husband had those eyes, too."

Rebecca was shaking her head. "No, you're wrong." She

moved closer, took Soula's hands in hers. "Look, this is going to come as a shock, but Fliss didn't love Damon. She loved someone else—"

"Oh, I know all that." Soula gave a dismissive wave of her hand.

"You know?" Rebecca stared. "But *how?*"

"I'm a mother. I knew that Fliss didn't love my son. But neither did he love her. Each had their own agenda for marrying—and, no, it wasn't love. I didn't approve. I was very disappointed with my eldest son's choice."

"T.J. is the son of—"

"Hush," said Soula. "Don't say anything that you will later regret. T.J. is Damon's son, and when you marry that will be final."

"No, we're not getting married." Rebecca shook her head at Soula's obstinacy but couldn't help feeling flattered that Soula wanted her in the family. "Thank you, Soula. But it won't work."

Soula sagged back on the sofa, her wrinkles deeper, looking every one of her years. "You know, I told that stubborn son of mine not to come back to Auckland without you. For once in his life he did what I asked. I think he was scared I was going to die. I wanted him to see you again and fall in love with you. I want grandchildren."

So Soula had been scheming. She hadn't been well, but she'd seen an opportunity to manipulate. A true Asteriades. The ends always justified the means. But Rebecca couldn't stir up any anger. Instead she gave the older woman a wan smile. "You are a truly wicked woman, but I wish you hadn't meddled."

"I wasn't well. I didn't lie about that." Soula tried to look righteous. Then she spoiled it by shooting Rebecca a guilty look. "There's something else I shouldn't have done, so I'm not even going to tell you about it, because it has the potential to make everything so much worse. I should've left everything well enough alone, never tried to get you two back together again."

"But then I wouldn't have gotten to see you again."

"Oh, Rebecca." Silver tears glistened in the corners of Soula's eyes. "You are the daughter I wish I had. So gracious, so loving."

Rebecca's own throat closed up. "You know, I don't really remember my mother. But in my dreams, she's you. But sometimes no amount of forcing will make something work if it's not meant to be." She bent and planted a kiss on Soula's forehead. "Damon and I, well, there is something between us, but we've agreed to give each other a little time and space. I'm going to miss you while I'm in Tohunga. But I will be back and I want you to promise not to interfere again. This is something that Damon and I must sort out, not a fairy godmother's wand."

"I won't meddle again. I promise. But that stubborn son of mine is headstrong. An idiot. And sometimes he needs a good old-fashioned kick up the pants."

Despite her misery, Rebecca couldn't help herself. She laughed.

It was Friday evening in Los Angeles—Saturday in Auckland. Instead of planning the coming week, as was his norm, Damon stood on the balcony of a hotel suite overlooking Santa Monica Bay, ten minutes away from the flurry of LAX. The continuous drone of planes over the Pacific held Damon transfixed. T.J. would've loved it. He stared west over the endless Pacific. Beyond Hawaii to the south lay New Zealand…and Rebecca.

What were Rebecca and T.J. doing? He couldn't stop thinking about Rebecca. The shock and fear that had flashed in her eyes when he'd said goodbye bothered him. She'd thought that he was leaving, telling her it was over. Was that what she expected? Did she think he'd make love to her like there was no tomorrow, then walk away at the first opportunity?

Perhaps she did.

When had he ever given her reason to think differently? She'd probably read his request for time as the precursor to his leaving. What had he ever done to deserve her trust?

The pain that had been kindling ignited into a burst of anguish. Four years ago he'd made a massive mistake. He'd picked the bride his brain told him he wanted. In his arrogance, he'd refused to see what Rebecca was. Even his mother had known.

He'd compounded his error in judgment by letting Rebecca slip through his fingers. Not because she was unsuitable, outrageous, manipulative. Despite all the things he'd told himself, he'd still wanted her, burned for her. And he'd driven her away with cold glares and cruel barbs.

Because of fear.

She terrified him. He shifted, uncomfortable with what he was forcing himself to admit.

He feared losing control of his inner self, of putting his heart and soul into the hands of a woman he couldn't bring himself to trust.

So he had run and married Rebecca's best friend to give his mother the grandchildren she craved. He married the wrong woman, for all the wrong reasons. And Fliss had married him for the wrong reasons, too. Both of them had done Rebecca a terrible injustice.

At Fliss's funeral he'd stared across the grave at Rebecca, humiliation scorching him. Yet despite the consuming fury there'd been a kind of relief.

His marriage had been wrong.

Fliss's death had freed him.

But it had been too soon for him to admit the enormity of his mistake—not that his arrogance would've let him. He'd allowed his mother to convince him to let Rebecca go, without taking revenge. Because deep down he'd known. He was the one who had screwed up.

Not Rebecca.

And he'd needed to come to terms with that.

Now he had. It had taken him all week to realise how brave people conquered fear. Rebecca's great overriding fear was losing a loved one. It was a real fear.

Damon balled his fists.

Rebecca had lost her parents. *Theos*, she'd never even had a chance to know her father. He uncurled two fingers and stared at them. Her brother and her best friend. Another two fingers unfurled. Aaron Grainger had committed suicide. He stared down at the five outstretched fingers of his right hand.

Five people. The five closest to her. Did her fear of loss stop her loving T.J.?

Of course not. She loved him. Recklessly. Incandescently. Tenderly. Without restraint or fear, Rebecca had raised her dead friend's baby. The child of the woman who had betrayed her. All Rebecca had done was give and give and give. No one gave her anything back.

She was so strong. She was even prepared to risk becoming his lover when she suspected that there was nothing down the road for her except rejection.

He was the coward. He'd never even told her how she made him feel. He'd told her that he needed time. Damon unrolled the index finger on his left hand and stared at his hands. Yes, Rebecca believed she'd lost him, too. If he wanted to be part of Rebecca's life, part of the family Rebecca had recreated, he had to act and overcome his fear.

Damon wheeled around and hurried into his suite.

His cell phone lay on the table in the sitting room. But Rebecca was not home. Demetra told him that she'd gone to Tohunga to check up on her business and she wasn't sure when Rebecca would be back. Damon disconnected and checked his watch. Rebecca would be at Chocolatique now. It would be better to say what needed to be said face-to-face.

The printout of his diary lay on the coffee table. The pages showed that the next month was hell. He frowned. He had to get through the next week here in L.A. But after that…

Picking up a fat gold pen, he slashed through his commitments for the last fortnight of the month. Everything would have to be rescheduled because he was taking two weeks off to invest in his future.

The next move was his.

Ten

It was Monday morning, eleven days after she had departed, that Rebecca drove back into the elegantly curved drive of the Asteriades mansion. For the last time, she promised herself.

T.J. was bubbling with excitement in the car seat behind her, his oblivious joy underscoring Rebecca's dread.

It had taken Rebecca two whole days to compose herself after the phone call she'd received from Soula on Friday evening. She still could hardly believe what Soula had told her. Yet she'd begged Soula to let her be the one to break the news to Damon. He deserved that much. Friday night had passed in a blur of tears. As the pale dawn had broken on Saturday, she'd decided what she had to do.

Yesterday had been heartbreaking. She'd taken T.J. down to their favourite rock pool at the beach. He'd paddled, knee-deep in the water, his fear slowly receding as he'd splashed around. With her digital camera she'd taken hundreds of photos. As if that would ever be enough.

In the afternoon they'd sat in the shade of the pohutukawa

tree in the front garden, and Rebecca had known that when the tree burst into flame-red flowers this Christmas she would not have the heart to sit beneath it. She would be struggling to put together the broken shards of her life.

The time had come to sell the house. She'd buy another, start afresh. Perhaps closer to Auckland. Chocolatique would have to go, too. Miranda and her sister had expressed interest in taking over the business. She'd start looking out for a new business opportunity. It would give her something to do to keep her mind off—

Soula opened the front door, interrupting her fragmented plans. Deep lines scored the older woman's cheeks. She'd aged. Rebecca saw from her face that Soula, too, knew this was the end. Wordlessly Rebecca walked into Soula's arms. They clutched each other and Soula's shoulders shook.

At last Rebecca stepped away. "Is Damon here?"

"His flight landed an hour ago. He should be home any minute." Soula's voice broke. "Come to my suite. I'll give you the report."

"Will you keep T.J. entertained until I've spoken to Damon?"

Soula nodded, her eyes wet with unshed tears.

When Damon strode into the lounge, Rebecca was waiting for him, outwardly composed but inwardly shaking. He'd already shed his jacket and pulled his tie loose and was in the act of unbuttoning the top buttons of his silk shirt when he saw her. A range of emotions flashed across his face. Rebecca thought she saw a glimpse of wonder and then it was gone and only astonishment remained.

"I thought you were in Tohunga?"

Rebecca rose to her quaking feet. "I've come to return your son."

"My son?" A frown creased his brow. "What do you mean?"

"T.J. is your son. Your mother had a DNA test done. She posted off samples of your hair and T.J.'s to some company in Australia a while ago—without my knowledge. However reprehensible her actions might've been, the results are pretty much conclusive. Here's the report." She thrust it into his hands. "He's your son. Yours and Fliss's."

Her eyes were filling with tears. Dear God, she wished she'd stop blubbering. "Damon, I swear I never knew." She stopped, swallowed, fighting to compose herself. "You'll find T.J.'s birth certificate in the envelope, too. Just before she died Fliss signed the application and stated in the declaration that James was the father."

Damon pulled the document out. "Tyler James. My son's name is Tyler James. Fliss always did say she wanted to call our son Tyler." His eyes were blank, shocked.

Remorse streamed into the empty hole in her heart. "I'm so sorry. I can't imagine how you must feel. I feel so *guilty*. The day after he was born I signed a declaration as James's kin confirming that he was James's son. I believed it. James believed it. But I can't forgive myself—because of me, you've lost out on time with your son, time you will never recover."

He didn't answer. He was still staring at the paper he held, the paper that listed her brother as T.J.'s father. What was he thinking? God, he must hate her. Unending questions spun through her mind. Had Fliss ever believed James to be her baby's father? Or had she known she was already pregnant, bearing Damon's child? Rebecca remembered the doctor saying after the birth that he would have said the baby was full-term—not premature at all. But she didn't even want to think about it. She'd never know for certain anyway.

"I'm sure you'll be able to get T.J.'s second name changed. And the father's name corrected," she babbled. "A court order will be easy enough to obtain with the DNA evidence."

What would her baby's name be? Not T.J. anymore. Damon would drop the James. He wouldn't want any reminders. Maybe he'd keep Tyler.

She didn't know what more she could do to make it right.

What would ever be enough? "I'll sign any documents you need me sign to relinquish my rights to Tyler."

"Relinquish your rights to Tyler?" Those startling blue eyes focused on her. "What are you talking about?"

"I'm talking about the fact that I adopted him. Maybe you'll want to change both his names on the certificate." Inside her heart ached with savage grief. "I'll do whatever I can to make it right, even though I can never give you back the missing years." With trembling fingers she wiped the fresh tears out her eyes. "All his stuff is upstairs, in the room I was using. He's going to need you. It will be difficult at first." Then she added in a rush, "I'd like to see him sometimes."

"What the hell do you mean?"

She could understand Damon's never wanting to set eyes on her again, not wanting her in T.J.'s life. But she needed that—she couldn't let T.J. go completely. She drew a deep breath. "I'm selling my house in Tohunga—and Chocolatique. I'll find something in Auckland, somewhere closer to—" *you and T.J.* "—T.J."

"You can stay here."

She went still. "I can't stay, Damon. He's your child."

He shook his head, looking stupefied. "But you're his mother."

She shook her head wildly. "No, I'm not. Fliss is his mother."

"You're his mother in every way that counts."

The pain nearly shattered her. "But you're his father, his real father. His place is with you." She'd have the memories of the years with T.J. as a baby, the memories of Damon's lovemaking to carry her through the rest of her life. Hopefully Damon would agree to visits, too. She'd see them maybe once a month. That would have to be enough.

He took a hesitant step toward her, then stopped. "You would do that? You'd give up the person you love more than your own life to me?"

"You belong together."

"You belong with us, too."

Her heart skipped. "What do you mean?"

"T.J. is your child." He moved quickly. Before she could blink, he had her in a rough bear hug. "I'm not letting you go. I love you," he whispered against her neck. "You're not going anywhere. I'm going to do what I should've done four years ago if I hadn't been so blind. I'm going to marry you."

She started to tremble. "You love me? You want to marry me?"

"Yes." He held her tighter, his arms hard bands around her ribs.

His throat was very smooth, very tanned, and she watched his Adam's apple move convulsively. "You don't even know if I love you," she murmured.

"You love me. If I wanted proof, you just gave it. You were prepared to leave T.J. with me, sign him over to me completely and go away. But I'm not letting you go. Never again."

"You're right, I love you." Rebecca pressed her lips against the hollow of his throat and then she whispered, "So what are you going to do about it?"

They tore off their clothes and fell on top of Damon's wide bed. Damon pulled Rebecca onto him, moaning as her naked skin slid across his torso.

She placed her lips over his, swallowing his next moan, and licked the slick heat of his mouth. The salty taste of her tears on his skin made her wipe the back of her hand across her face.

"Let me," he whispered, the sound husky in the silent room. His thumbs stroked across her eyes, closing them, the pads soft against her eyelids.

When she opened her eyes again, she stared down into his and asked, "Do you forgive me?"

"What for?" His expression held bewilderment.

"For keeping your son from you."

He stilled. "You didn't know he was my son. And you

raised him with love, lots of love, without holding back an‹
never hesitated risking your heart. You kept him safe. How ca›
I ever hold that against you?"

"Thank heavens." Relief washed through her, turning he›
knees weak. "When Soula, called I was so afraid—"

"Don't." He pulled her close. "I don't want you to ever b‹
afraid again. We have so much for which to be grateful. I mus›
have done something good in my life to have got this..
you...right."

She made a sound that was half laugh, half choke. "I'm fa›
from perfect, you know."

"You're perfect for me." His hand smoothed over the bac›
of her thigh, over the curve of her buttock. She murmure‹
something incomprehensible as his fingers traced up th›
groove of her spine. Shivered.

Then his hands laced into her hair. He held her fast. H‹
pulled her down and opened his mouth as their lips met, hi›
tongue surging into her mouth. The kiss was ravenous.

Rebecca scissored her legs against his, then let them par›
falling on either side of his thighs, and she pressed herse›
against him.

He shuddered.

His hands loosened and he fell back against the pillows.

Rebecca wriggled a little, rubbed against his hardness an‹
watched the blaze of heat light his eyes.

"Rebecca. Oh, Rebecca." His voice was throaty. "Neve›
leave me."

"Never! I'll keep you close. Forever." She shot him a litt›
grin. Shifted her lower body over a fraction. Felt his erectio›
leap. Then she moved.

"Woman, what are you doing?"

But he knew.

His face was alight. She stared down at him. There wa›
desire and passion in his face, but more than that, there wa›
love. Naked, unashamed love.

For her.

It turned her on.

She raised her hips carefully, slowly, conscious of the length of him below her. Her body was already slick with arousal. His hand was moving downward.

"No."

He froze at her command.

"Keep still. Watch me. I want to love you."

His eyes never wavered from hers. "I love you more than I've loved any woman. Do you know that? I love everything about you. I wouldn't change anything about who you are, how you make me feel. I've never felt anything like this before."

Rebecca stared into the deep blue depths. The black streaks like dark, dangerous rocks in a tempestuous sea. "I believe you."

She paused for a heartbeat.

Then she sank down with one swift movement, sheathing him within her heat. There was a moment of sheer pleasure...and a warm glow of completion. She watched emotion explode in his eyes until the blue burned like silver. Wonder, pleasure and more love.

His arms wrapped around her shoulders, pulling her down against him. A moment later he began to rock his hips. Skin slid against skin. Slowly. So, so slowly. The pleasure that burst through her was incredible.

She gave herself up to the wildness, the heat.

When they finally gained track of time, Damon and Rebecca came downstairs to announce that they would be getting married. There was jubilation and Soula wept a little with joy.

Finally everyone settled down to dinner and Rebecca gazed around the faces at the table: Soula, Demetra, Savvas, T.J. *Her family*. Her own eyes prickled with tears of happiness. So many people, so much love. When her gaze came around to the man seated beside her, he gave her a slow, satisfied smile.

"So who gets to plan your wedding, Rebecca?" Demetra chimed in.

"I'll take care of that," Damon said firmly. "I think I know what the bride's fantasies are." His smile grew wide and Rebecca eyed the curve of that sexy lower lip with hunger. Beneath the table his hand moved in lazy circles against her thigh. Rebecca shot him a narrow glance.

Demetra started to laugh. "Well, this is one marriage no one needs to worry about. You two are so in tune it's positively scary."

"About time they realised it," Soula snorted.

"If Mummy marries Daddy, does that mean I get ducks?" T.J. piped, tugging at Damon's sleeve.

"Whatever you want—"

"Let's think about it, okay?" Rebecca interrupted Damon, rolling her eyes. "Ducks in the lap pool? I can see that you're going to take full advantage of the situation, young man."

T.J. gave a naughty grin. "But I've never had a Daddy."

Damon's eyes flared hot with emotion as he looked from T.J. to Rebecca. "I've never had a son. And soon I'll have a wife. What more could any man ask?"

Later, back in Damon's bed, their bodies a naked tangle under the covers, Damon murmured, "I meant every word."

Rebecca nestled closer. T.J. was fast asleep a couple of doors down in his new room, the room Rebecca had occupied before. Damon's hand stroked her shoulder, then disappeared under the covers to caress the smooth skin of her back. Heat followed where his fingers touched. She shifted.

His hand stilled. "Can you ever forgive me?"

She lifted her head, stared down at him. In the dim gold of the bedside light she saw that his face was relaxed, his mouth tender.

"Forgive you for what?"

"T.J. should have been your son."

She brushed back the lock that had fallen across his

forehead. "He is my son. In every way that matters." She kissed his cheek. "And how could I not forgive you? You forgave me for keeping T.J. away from you."

"You did that unknowingly."

"You believe me?"

He gave her a content, trusting smile. "Of course."

She settled down beside him. "I can't tell you what your belief means to me."

He turned his head on the pillow beside hers and met her eyes. "Why does it mean so much?"

"I feel like I'm always fighting what people believe." She paused. "It wasn't true, you know."

He hooked his arm around her, drew her close to his side until he felt her grow warm from his heat. "What wasn't true?"

"That Aaron left me a fortune and I squandered it. Aaron committed suicide because he'd been caught with his hand in the till, he'd defrauded the bank to the tune of millions. Naturally the bank didn't want the news to get out—bad publicity, the impact on the share prices and all that." Curling up in his arms, she said, "He didn't even tell me what he'd done. I knew something was wrong, but I never dreamed it was that."

Damon hugged her tightly. How could Grainger have messed it up? The man had had it all. Money. Success. And, above all, Rebecca. Damon knew he could afford to be gracious. "He was a good man. But his position must have offered temptations he was incapable of resisting. And once he was found out, well, he would never have wanted you to see him in trouble."

Damon suspected Aaron Grainger had liked the godlike status he'd achieved. He wouldn't have wanted a life without the patina wealth brought, without the status. The sneers during a trial, the snubs when he came out of prison would've destroyed Grainger.

"After his death—" Rebecca broke off and gave a shiver.

"It was months of hell. Aaron had opened heaven knows how many offshore accounts and siphoned the funds out the country. I gave the bank all the help I could. They repossessed fixed assets, liquidated everything. He should've told me. I would've stood by him."

Damon shook his head and stroked slow fingers down her back. He didn't doubt that Rebecca would've stood by her husband. Aaron Grainger had left his young bride to face the heat, and taken the coward's way out. And she still didn't denounce him.

What kind of woman was she? A saint?

Shame seeped through Damon. He'd heard the stories, been eager to believe them. Now he'd discovered the truth. She hadn't squandered Aaron's ill-gotten fortune, she hadn't driven him to suicide. She'd respected her dead husband's memory, had never sledged him off to anyone.

He kissed the top of her head. "I've told you before that Aaron recognised your worth. Infinitely precious."

Her head came up and she gave him a grateful smile. "Thank you for that. Aaron was very good to me."

He wasn't going to argue. The man was dead. No threat to what they shared. And he could never forget that Aaron Grainger had taken a chance on him and helped him when Stellar International had been in trouble. Aaron had played an important role in both their lives. He deserved to be remembered. Damon stared into the dark, slanting eyes that did such dangerous things to his equilibrium. He swallowed. "You must wear the pendant he chose for you. It suits you."

Her face lit up. "You wouldn't mind?"

He hesitated, then said firmly, "Of course not."

"This sounds awful, but I have to tell you—it's my favourite piece of jewellery."

Damn, he'd be reminded of Aaron Grainger every day of his life if she wore it. Then he pushed away the tiny sliver of resentment. Rebecca was the woman she was today because of her past. Earlier he'd told her he loved everything about her, that he wouldn't change anything about who she was. Every word had been true. She was complex, caring and much more woman than he deserved. If the pendant gave her happiness, he would never object to her wearing it. "It suits you. Grainger had good taste," he said gruffly.

"I used to wear it a lot."

"I remember."

"At first I wore it to remind me of Aaron." For an instant she looked apprehensive. Then she said in a rush, "After I met you, I wore it because the colour always reminded me of your eyes."

God. She never ceased to surprise him. But he was thankful he'd told her how much he loved her before this final bastion had fallen. Her arms crept around his neck and pulled him close. The kiss he placed on her mouth was long and lingering. Her lips parted and he deepened the kiss. Heat rose swiftly within him. After a few minutes, he raised his head and muttered hoarsely, "I don't deserve your love. I don't deserve a second chance."

"Watch it, you're talking about the man I love." She reared up on her elbow.

"When we first met, I looked at you, wanted you…but I was a coward. I saw all your passion, your intensity, and turned and ran instead of sweeping up the challenge you presented. I would've received riches beyond measure. Instead I retreated, threw Felicity in your face as the model for womanhood. You say I'm blind. I'm not. I'm stupid."

"You're not stupid. Fliss was a darling."

"Loyal to the last, aren't you?" He brushed her hair back from her face. "I married her for all the wrong reasons. Because my mother wanted grandchildren. Because she was biddable. Because she was so different from you, she didn't tie my head— or my heart—in knots. But I came to wish she had a little of your steel." As he admitted the truth, the shame started to recede.

"Fliss was weak. But it's not her fault. Not wholly. She had a hard time."

"She had you. Yet she married the man you wanted, left you to look after the man she loved—and still you defend her."

"I must. I loved her. And she gave me T.J."

"Our son."

"Yes, our son. Now I've got you. And you love me. What more could I want?" She smiled at him, a slow smile. A happy smile filled with promise.

Damon leaned forward and gave her a gentle kiss, thankful that he'd found her again. The woman who loved him more than he deserved. The woman who bewitched him. The woman who held his heart in her hands.

Two weeks later and a world away from the bustle of Auckland, a lone couple stood on the wide strip of golden sand. The woman's feet were bare and damp from the surf, and she was clad in a simple long white dress. A blue opal pendant hung from a gold chain that glinted in the late-afternoon sun. And she wore a brand-new set of matching earings and a bracelet that her bridegroom had given her as a wedding present. The groom wore a light-coloured suit fitting for the island's humidity, and the page boy wore a pair of floral board shorts and a dun-coloured shirt.

There were no bridal attendants, no guests, no hoopla. Only a bride, her groom and their son. As the celebrant walked toward them with two women who had agreed to act as witnesses, the groom leaned down. "Is a Pacific island close enough to your fantasy?"

The bride tipped her head up. "I don't need anything beside you—and our son."

"You're sure you don't feel cheated of the celebration, the guests, the presents?"

Rebecca laughed. "Believe me, there will be mountains of presents to open when we fly home—between your mother and Demetra, I don't doubt that. But I've had the best gifts already. You, the fact that T.J. swam today and that he laughed while doing it."

The groom cupped her face in both his hands and stared down at her with gleaming blue eyes, his touch warm and tender. She turned her head and kissed the arch of his thumb. Never had she been happier.

"I love you," Damon told her, his voice fierce. "Have I told you today?"

"Yes, but I'll never tire of hearing it."

"And I'll never tire of the wonder of finding you and my son" He bent to kiss her.

Rebecca's toes curled into the soft sand. The familiar flare of desire flickered within her. The celebrant gave a cough. For a moment Rebecca thought Damon was going to ignore the man. Then he murmured, "Later" against her lips and drew away. The wide white pirate smile he flashed her held a promise that made her tingle.

"Dearly beloved," the celebrant intoned. "We are gathered here today to celebrate a wedding, the love of two people for each other…"

Soula Asteriades smiled from ear to ear as she made her way to the deck where the sound of festivities could be heard.

Her eldest spinster sister, Iphegenia, was ensconced in a large comfortable chair with plenty of cushions supporting her. The younger, Athina, was playing *tavli* with Johnny. Soula's three brothers and their wives and children and grandchildren were scattered across the deck, some of the little ones playing in the peculiar long, skinny pool her son had built. Savvas and his bride-to-be shared a lounger, their heads close together like a pair of lovebirds.

"Look, a photo," Soula announced, holding up a cell phone. "The first photo of my eldest son, his new bride wearing a beautiful white dress—no sign of scarlet in sight—and their son, my first grandson. This is a miracle for which I claim no responsibility."

As the family surged forward, happiness swamped her. She tilted her face to the heavens and knew somewhere out there her beloved Ari was watching, celebrating with her.

* * * * *

Don't miss Tessa Radley's next release,
RICH MAN'S REVENGE,
available in June from Silhouette Desire.

Set in darkness beyond the ordinary world.
Passionate tales of life and death.
With characters' lives ruled by laws the everyday
world can't begin to imagine.

n●cturne

It's time to discover the Raintree trilogy...

New York Times bestselling author
LINDA HOWARD
brings you the dramatic first book
RAINTREE: INFERNO

The Ansara Wizards are rising and the Raintree clan
must rejoin the battle against their foes,
testing their powers, relationships and
forcing upon them lives they never
could have imagined before...

Turn the page for a sneak preview
of the captivating first book
in the Raintree trilogy,
RAINTREE: INFERNO
by LINDA HOWARD
On sale April 25

Dante Raintree stood with his arms crossed as he watched the woman on the monitor. The image was in black and white to better show details; color distracted the brain. He focused on her hands, watching every move she made, but what struck him most was how uncommonly *still* she was. She didn't fidget or play with her chips, or look around at the other players. She peeked once at her down card, then didn't touch it again, signaling for another hit by tapping a fingernail on the table. Just because she didn't seem to be paying attention to the other players, though, didn't mean she was as unaware as she seemed.

"What's her name?" Dante asked.

"Lorna Clay," replied his chief of security, Al Rayburn. "At first I thought she was counting, but she doesn't pay enough attention."

"She's paying attention, all right," Dante murmured. "You just don't see her doing it." A card counter had to remember every card played. Supposedly counting cards was impossible with the number of decks used by the casinos, but there were those rare individuals who could calculate the odds even with multiple decks.

"I thought that, too," said Al. "But look at this piece of tape coming up. Someone she knows comes up to her and speaks, she looks around and starts chatting, completely misses the play of the people to her left—and doesn't look around even when the deal comes back to her, just taps that finger. And damn if she didn't win. Again."

Dante watched the tape, rewound it, watched it again. Then he watched it a third time. There had to be something he was missing, because he couldn't pick out a single giveaway.

"If she's cheating," Al said with something like respect, "she's the best I've ever seen."

"What does your gut say?"

Al scratched the side of his jaw, considering. Finally, he said, "If she isn't cheating, she's the luckiest person walking. She wins. Week in, week out, she wins. Never a huge amount, but I ran the numbers and she's into us for about five grand a week. Hell, boss, on her way out of the casino she'll stop by a slot machine, feed a dollar in and walk away with at least fifty. It's never the same machine, either. I've had her watched, I've had her followed, I've even looked for the same faces in the casino every time she's in here, and I can't find a common denominator."

"Is she here now?"

"She came in about half an hour ago. She's playing blackjack, as usual."

"Bring her to my office," Dante said, making a swift decision. "Don't make a scene."

"Got it," said Al, turning on his heel and leaving the security center.

Dante left, too, going up to his office. His face was calm. Normally he would leave it to Al to deal with a cheater, but he was curious. How was she doing it? There were a lot o bad cheaters, a few good ones, and every so often one would come along who was the stuff of which legends were made: the cheater who didn't get caught, even when people were alert and the camera was on him—or, in this case, her.

It was possible to simply be lucky, as most people understood luck. Chance could turn a habitual loser into a big-time winner. Casinos, in fact, thrived on that hope. But luck itself wasn't habitual, and he knew that what passed for luck was often something else: cheating. And there was the other kind of luck, the kind he himself possessed, but it depended not on chance but on who and what he was. He knew it was an innate power and not Dame Fortune's erratic smile. Since power like his was rare, the odds made it likely the woman he'd been watching was merely a very clever cheat.

Her skill could provide her with a very good living, he thought, doing some swift calculations in his head. Five grand a week equaled $260,000 a year, and that was just from his casino. She probably hit them all, careful to keep the numbers relatively low so she stayed under the radar.

He wondered how long she'd been taking him, how long she'd been winning a little here, a little there, before Al noticed.

The curtains were open on the wall-to-wall window in his office, giving the impression, when one first opened the door, of stepping out onto a covered balcony. The glazed window faced west, so he could catch the sunsets. The sun was low now, the sky painted in purple and gold. At his home in the mountains, most of the windows faced east, affording him views of the sunrise. Something in him needed both the greeting and the goodbye of the sun. He'd always been drawn to sunlight, maybe because fire was his element to call, to control.

He checked his internal time: four minutes until sundown. Without checking the sunrise tables every day, he knew exactly when the sun would slide behind the mountains. He didn't own an alarm clock. He didn't need one. He was so acutely attuned to the sun's position that he had only to check within himself to know the time. As for waking at a particular time, he was one of those people who could tell himself to wake at a certain time, and he did. That talent had nothing to do with being a Raintree, so he didn't have to hide it; a lot of perfectly ordinary people had the same ability.

He had other talents and abilities, however, that did require careful shielding. The long days of summer instilled in him an almost sexual high, when he could feel contained power buzzing just beneath his skin. He had to be doubly careful not to cause candles to leap into flame just by his presence, or to start wildfires with a glance in the dry-as-tinder brush. He loved Reno; he didn't want to burn it down. He just felt so damn *alive* with all the sunshine pouring down that he wanted to let the energy pour through him instead of holding it inside.

This must be how his brother Gideon felt while pulling lightning, all that hot power searing through his muscles, his veins. They had this in common, the connection with raw power. All the members of the far-flung Raintree clan had some power, some heightened ability, but only members of the royal family could channel and control the earth's natural energies.

Dante wasn't just of the royal family, he was the Dranir, the leader of the entire clan. "Dranir" was synonymous with king, but the position he held wasn't ceremonial, it was one of sheer power. He was the oldest son of the previous Dranir, but he would have been passed over for the position if he hadn't also inherited the power to hold it.

Behind him came Al's distinctive knock on the door. The outer office was empty, Dante's secretary having gone home hours before. "Come in," he called, not turning from his view of the sunset.

The door opened, and Al said, "Mr. Raintree, this is Lorna Clay."

Dante turned and looked at the woman, all his senses on alert. The first thing he noticed was the vibrant color of her hair, a rich, dark red that encompassed a multitude of shades from copper to burgundy. The warm amber light danced along the iridescent strands, and he felt a hard tug of sheer lust in his gut. Looking at her hair was almost like looking at fire, and he had the same reaction.

The second thing he noticed was that she was spitting mad.

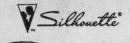

REQUEST YOUR FREE BOOKS!

2 FREE NOVELS PLUS 2 FREE GIFTS!

Silhouette® Desire®

Passionate, Powerful, Provocative!

YES! Please send me 2 FREE Silhouette Desire® novels and my 2 FREE gifts. After receiving them, if I don't wish to receive any more books, I can return the shipping statement marked "cancel." If I don't cancel, I will receive 6 brand-new novels every month and be billed just $3.80 per book in the U.S., or $4.47 per book in Canada, plus 25¢ shipping and handling per book and applicable taxes, if any*. That's a savings of almost 15% off the cover price! I understand that accepting the 2 free books and gifts places me under no obligation to buy anything. I can always return a shipment and cancel at any time. Even if I never buy another book from Silhouette, the two free books and gifts are mine to keep forever.   225 SDN EEXJ 326 SDN EEXU

Name _____ (PLEASE PRINT) _____

Address _____ Apt. _____

City _____ State/Prov. _____ Zip/Postal Code _____

Signature (if under 18, a parent or guardian must sign)

Mail to the **Silhouette Reader Service™:**
IN U.S.A.: P.O. Box 1867, Buffalo, NY 14240-1867
IN CANADA: P.O. Box 609, Fort Erie, Ontario L2A 5X3

Not valid to current Silhouette Desire subscribers.

Want to try two free books from another line?
Call 1-800-873-8635 or visit www.morefreebooks.com.

* Terms and prices subject to change without notice. NY residents add applicable sales tax. Canadian residents will be charged applicable provincial taxes and GST. This offer is limited to one order per household. All orders subject to approval. Credit or debit balances in a customer's account(s) may be offset by any other outstanding balance owed by or to the customer. Please allow 4 to 6 weeks for delivery.

Your Privacy: Silhouette is committed to protecting your privacy. Our Privacy Policy is available online at www.eHarlequin.com or upon request from the Reader Service. From time to time we make our lists of customers available to reputable firms who may have a product or service of interest to you. If you would prefer we not share your name and address, please check here. ☐

SDES07

Silhouette®

Romantic
SUSPENSE

**Sparked by Danger,
Fueled by Passion.**

*This month and every month look for
four new heart-racing romances
set against a backdrop of suspense!*

Available in May 2007

Safety in Numbers
(Wild West Bodyguards miniseries)
by **Carla Cassidy**

Jackson's Woman
by **Maggie Price**

Shadow Warrior
(Night Guardians miniseries)
by **Linda Conrad**

One Cool Lawman
by **Diane Pershing**

Available wherever you buy books!

Visit Silhouette Books at www.eHarlequin.com

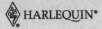